GW00499149

Writers of Ottery

Anthology

Anthology

Writers of Ottery

Anthology

Contents

Photography © Graham Bishop

Foreword

Writers of Ottery

We are a group of East Devon writers who love writing. That doesn't mean we are very good at it or do it all the time, but attempting to put the right words in the best order is something that energises us and spurs us on.

Devon is a renowned centre for creativity and writing.

Writers of Ottery

Ottery itself has a long literary tradition. Back in the early Middle Ages the parish church of St Mary, once a Collegiate Church with a fine library until Henry VIII's dissolution in 1545, produced such writers as Alexander Barclay who wrote, The Ship of Fools (1509). Later there was Samuel Taylor Coleridge (b 1772) whose romantic and poetic works reflect the enchantment of the place of his birth. More recently JK Rowling's Harry Potter stories contain links with Ottery. Is it then surprising we find this an inspirational place?

The present Writers Group is a child of the millennium and first began meeting formally from around 2013, meeting monthly on Monday evenings over hot drinks, first at Seasons Tea Rooms, then when Covid struck, all gatherings ceased. As restrictions lifted, we then met at the Ottery Hub before settling in our current venue - the Town Council Meeting Room.

There are some 40+ people who are closely or lightly attached to our group, and we are a very mixed bunch. Some have yet to write but want to write, some have dipped a literary toe in the water, whilst others have pushed on to write poetry, children's books, cookery books, family memoirs, non-fiction or all manner of fiction.

We held our first Literary Festival in the town in October 2022 to coincide with Coleridge's 250th birthday and this Anthology, with articles by some of our group has been our latest project. More information is on our website: https://otterywriters.wordpress.com

If you would like to join us, contact me through:
otterybooks@btinternet.com
We hope you enjoy this collection of our writing, some with links to our town, others with personal stories to tell.

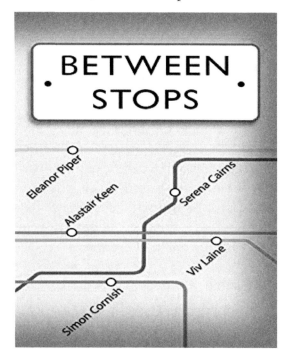

Back in the day, in 2014 under Simon Cornish's guidance our first anthology called 'Between Stops' was collated and published containing 37 short stories which can be read between stops on the London Underground.

Message from the Ottery St Mary Library

The whole team at Ottery St Mary Library feel honoured that the Ottery Writers Group have asked us to write a foreword to this book and that the writers' group are kindly donating the profits to our library. Our library is one of the 54 libraries run by the charity Libraries Unlimited across Devon and Torbay, and every donation helps us continue to enrich people's lives and build thriving communities.

We could talk in detail about Ottery library and the work that we do, however as this information is available on our website, we have instead decided to share some quotes and feedback from our lovely customers.

"My favourite place is the library! I don't know what I'd do without you."

"I can't thank you enough, you have got my sporty, out-doorsy, mud splattered little boy excited about reading, it's fabulous."

"We love our library."

"I really appreciate all you and your team do both my children love reading books and the library really enriches their knowledge and understanding with the variety and quality of books."

"We are so lucky in Ottery having a great team at our library."

Anthology

We hope you enjoy this variety of works by local writers, and we look forward to welcoming you into our library soon!

Kerry Carr, Library Supervisor, Ottery St Mary Library

01404 813838

www.librariesunlimited.org.uk

1.
Blackbird Woken

Ruth MacGregor

Up early
blackbird woken
songs of the dawn
call me here.
Misty morn
cool and fresh
burbling brook
music making.
Pale pink light
ducks in flight
cattle drinking
at nights end

Waiting watching
listening, looking
hearing, seeing
cool breeze feeling.

Mist now clearing
now reappearing
wafting wraith like
above stream and field.
Lighter now
pink hues fade
dark diminishes

colours appear
shafts of sunlight
pierce the morning
golden rays
fresh and bright.
Darkness flees
light is stronger
with light comes hope
and fears diminish.
The welcome of the wild ones
birdsong and creatures call
the dawn of a new day.

Photography © Cynthea Gregory

Writers of Ottery

Photography © Graham Bishop

2.
The Statue

Grenville Gilbert

On the 21st October,
twenty twenty-two,
the statue was unveiled;
its first time on view.
Samuel's very birthday;
two-fifty he'd have been.
Born in the schoolhouse,
just yards from the scene.
Philosopher, poet, fell walker;
first to say 'mountaineer'.
Habituated to the vast;
a dreamer, it was clear.
Books are still being written
about this deep feeling man.
Christianity, not some theory
but, for him, a living plan.
Now in Ottery's churchyard,
on the grass on which he trod,
stands Samuel Taylor Coleridge,
a man, most honest to God.

3.
Lament of Coleridge's Wife

Melanie Barrow

Toil from day to dusk I do, in this damp, rat-infested cottage. Yet *he* grandly announced that *he'd* keep no servant, *he'd* work hard tending the pig, gardening, cooking. Huh! Fancy words. Oh yes, he's good at those, but it's me that's left working till my back aches.

Rest, that's what he does best, lying in bed all day with some illness or other, drinking that poison, which those Wordsworths say fuels his creativity. *I* can read, *I* can speak French, *I* can write, *I* was proficient in mathematics. Does he ever consider that *I* might like to sit at a desk and scribble about the baby at midnight instead of changing and feeding it? How can *I* rest when there's water to fetch, meat to be taken to the baker to cook, the pig to feed, and now even a lodger to care for?

Artists like him don't earn a regular wage. 'Get a proper job,' I implore, 'so I can pay the tradesmen's bills – poems don't pay them.' If only he were more like that nice Mr Poole, so courteous and friendly and with such a lovely house and library. 'Help yourself' he said to me – not just to Samuel. Those Wordsworths never talk to me like that, I'm just their skivvy. He does such a lot for the village too, setting up the women's society and a bank and school too.

Politics and Pantisocracy! That's why we met and why I suppose Sam married me in the end, so he could follow his utopian ideals – his big American dream. It seemed so exciting then.

Philosophy he wants to study now. So, he's off to tour Germany, spending the Wedgwoods' annuity and leaving me behind nursing the new baby. Doesn't he think I'd love to go too? There was a time when Robert Southey and I discussed philosophy. Perhaps I should have married him instead of Sam, and then I'd have my own house, like my sister.

Edifying he says it will be. Oh yes, but it doesn't put food on the table, does it? I'm lonely here in this hovel with nothing to do for fun. Stowey's not exactly Bath – how I miss it, and the fashionable clothes. If only father hadn't gone bankrupt. But then what does it matter? I won't have time to do anything other than chores anyway.

Death of our baby wasn't enough to bring you home then? Why didn't you hurry back, instead of taking a five-month walking holiday? I had no husband to comfort me, share my grief. Nine months I watched over him. The responsibility of his life weighed so heavily upon me, and now, despite my care, he's gone. My beautiful brown hair all fell out and I must needs wear this wig. Oh, where are you? Once you wrote: 'I'm married to the woman I love best of all Created Beings.' How easily you've forgotten. Oh, how you've left me trapped.

4.
Time and Space

Tony Dowling

Thoughts and Opinions
Stephen Hawking Inspires
Data is a Power (Just a thought).
Thoughts and Opinions compare

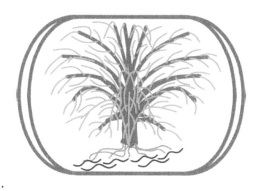

.

Thoughts

Thoughts   Thoughts   Thoughts

Thoughts   Thoughts   Thoughts   Thoughts
Thoughts

Anthology

Thoughts   Thoughts   Thoughts   Thoughts
Thoughts

Thoughts   Thoughts

Time and Space

Opinions

Opinions   Opinions   Opinions

Opinions   Opinions   Opinions   Opinions
Opinions

Opinions   Opinions   Opinions   Opinions
Opinions   Opinions   Opinions

Time and Space
Thoughts are Singularities.

Writers of Ottery

Thoughts are made to form atoms.

Thoughts gather to form Opinions.

Opinions convey thoughts.

Opinions gather to form Minds.

Thoughts and opinions are all unique.

Opinions travel in the form of data.

Singularities travel in the form of space dust.

Sand travels in the form of grains.

Thoughts travel in the form of singularities.

Minds travel as opinions.

We send data around the universe.
It can be transmitted and received in many ways.
Past, Present and Future.

Data is a power.

Power to the people ??????

Opinions which become truth are hopefully good and
benefit the world.

Anthology

Opinions which become truth might be bad and not benefit the world.

Whether they are as data or as atoms((or grains of sand) assembled in human form).

What we believe of our opinions is important.

Belief is important.

We need belief.

Some humans believe that the creator walked amongst us in human form.

That mass of atoms in human form told us that it is love and not power that drives the universe.

The heavenly bodies and stars of a universe supernova, black hole, and collapse into an atom.

That atom is a heavenly body, like a piece of sand floating in the universe.

When we split that atom (for power) we release all the archived power held in it.

When we frack (for power) we split atoms.

Writers of Ottery

Do we believe that this is a good thing to do??????????

Those atoms may be required as primers for a greater cause in creation.

Only the creator knows.

What name do we give to this creator?????

It is all about science or belief.

Singularities combining or Opinions forming beliefs to form our universe.

Isn't it a wonderful place to be!!!!

Thoughts and Opinions
Stephen Hawking Inspires
Data is a Power (Just a thought).
Thoughts and Opinions compare.

This piece to be read in conjunction with the following piece "Belief"

5.
Belief

A R Dowling

Helping see the wood from the trees

My father sat in a class at Brixham a good few years before Neil Armstrong walked on the moon. His teacher said.

"I believe that in your lifetime we will see a man walking on the moon".

There was a film which showed some people in a rocket going up to the moon at about the same time. Years later these beliefs (or opinions) were proven correct. The human race constructed a rocket and spaceship capable of transporting men to the moon.

Where did these thoughts come from???? For sure the beliefs and opinions of the people involved manifested in the crafting of the future.

So do we have the key to our future in our hands? Can

we manipulate our own destinies?

The Indigenous people of North America, ((Or Red Indians as they were once referred to) I would not mind the latter if I were an Indian), believe that we construct our lives in our sleep, dreaming of what we do during the day. Our hours awake are purely living the life we have already foreseen.

These beliefs, opinions, dreams all go towards forming a consciousness.

Some people write down what they think are the ways of the consciousness, they give names to iconic figures who champion the way forward for the human race.

Religious people believe in God and Jesus and some believe in other forms of consciousness (Religions).

Scientists believe in space, time, and heavenly bodies. (Religiously believing that we live in an ever expanding universe. Do we????, where is the end????).

Some people believe in both.

Only the truth matters.

Only the matter is truth.

Humans play with words, to impress their opinions and form their beliefs.

Nobody has an answer for space, time or heavenly bodies we only have belief for what they are.

But we know we live a life, and there is no greater gift than that of time.

Past, present, and future.

How we use that time is down to the validity of our beliefs.

6.
All Types of Taffeta

Mary Hewlett

Grey silk taffeta doesn't suit everybody.

It's fine if it's on royalty. The Countess of Wessex has worn it in a variety of styles, all very successfully. The 1950's tea length apparel suits her very well and, of course she has the poise and elegance and holds her head up beautifully.

But…anyone with wide hips and a slouch and you're talking about big attractions at London Zoo, and I'm not meaning the gazelles.

I had a lady this morning. With her daughter who had freckles but pretty enough.
Bride had opted for a very plain chiffon job, not from me.

But I never judge other people's choices. That wouldn't be professional. She showed me some photos on her phone.

I said "Oh, don't you look lovely!" Cleopatra has always been one of my favourite films, although of course Elizabeth Taylor was a stunning brunette, not a redhead.

"Yes, very lovely, dear."

Very brave.

Anyway, Mother chips in that she's looking for something for The Big Day.

She's a redhead too with touches of grey. I expect she'll get her roots done by then.

A Big, but quite stylish lady in her own country bumpkin sort of way.

I suggest a Cobalt Blue, with built in upholstery and gentle ruffles.

I find a matching hat (saucer but not overwhelming) and really, the effect is very pleasing.

I have shoes and a bag (with gold chain strap) that I discreetly lay on the chaise lounge nearby, just to entice.

I'm never pushy. Always professional.

Well, she turns this way and that and I can see that she's not blown away. Heavens knows why because that's the best she's ever going to look.

I keep my smile professionally beaming.

"Oh Madam I said what a picture!"

But no, she's got her heart set on a grey taffeta off the shoulder with detachable netted underskirt.

Plus a hat large enough to take ET home.

Swamps her.

But £500 more than the blue so I keep mum and display the accessories, (matching and contrast.)

She pumps for a flat heeled sandal. Says she wants to be comfortable.

I thought 'My dear you're not doing a ten hour shift at the library, go for elegance'.

But instead I say, "Oh Madam you'll stop traffic. I believe Princess Margaret enjoyed footwear of a similar style."

She said, "Oh Anastasia Armstrong-Jones? Are you related?"

I smile serenely. "Madam, I couldn't possibly comment. Discretion is my bible."

I can see she's impressed.

"And Anastasia?" She continues, "like the Russian

princess?" (Well, she's possibly more educated than she looks.)

I shrug my shoulders and say, "Oh well these family names get passed down….."

Mother says, "Oh my goodness. Is that why your shop is so much more expensive than everywhere else in town?"

"Quality. Quality. Quality, madam," I remind her.

"Every crystal is hand sewn. All of my designs are exclusive. Each one is an inspired creation. When I designed for…

"Well I can't mention names of course but they say Anastasia you were born with style and class running through your veins, along with your blue blood….!'"

Mother is awestruck with admiration.
Close up, I can see that her chin hairs need plucking.

And those earrings have a whiff of internet about them.

My Afternoon Booking is a bride wanting a beaded strapless over a very hefty bosom. Definitely not real. Put it this way, if she ever got caught in a monsoon, she'd never drown.

Arms covered in tattoos. I said, "Heavens, someone's been busy with the felt tips." But she seems rather proud of them. I suggested a french lace bolero just to give a little more coverage, and in my opinion some much needed decorum but the young miss declined.

"Lady Frederick Windsor wore one when she married at Hampton Court Palace. Very pleasing to the eye."

Once I'd laced up Miss Ski Slopes into the dress, her cleavage became even more pronounced. Sir Edmund Hilary would have been lost down there for months, no matter how many ropes and pulleys he had.

Indecent.

But of course I don't say that, always professional.

And she seems delighted with the result. Dress with crystal tiara and the crystal enchanted cathedral veil and she happily spends over three thousand.

I say, "It's very unusual to have a bride coming in alone."

She shrugs: "Mum wanted me to dress like Kate. And I'm like no way!"

I bristle slightly. "The Princess of Wales is a very stylish young lady but you my dear, have found your very own individual style. What about bridesmaids?"

"All sorted," she beams and shows me a picture.

Well…..all different shapes and sizes, could have been Russian dolls. Decked out in embellished maroon. Suited about two out of the eight. (The others needed body-wear, a health spa and in some cases a gastric band.)

In my experience, it's very unkind to put them in matching attire. Some, believe me, do not compare well.

All of them though have the most extraordinary eyelashes, even just to try on dresses. I'm all for high maintenance , (obviously you can see that) but nowadays it's Barbie Dolls R Us. With that lot, less eyelash extensions and more Spanx.

For natural and regal beauty you only have to look to The Duchess of Kent (married York Minister 1961). Radiant. Dignified. Some lipstick and a powder compact. Stunning. Swan like.

I'm just about to close for the day when Reg bangs on the door. "Parcels for you, Annie," he yells.

"I told you not to deliver till after 7, Reginald!"

"Well I need the space in the kitchen cos I'm taking the bike apart tonight and thought you'd be pissed if oil goes on these wedding dresses and all."

"Will you please keep your voice down ? Just drop them in the foyer thank you."

"Tell me," says Reg, bringing in several large boxes. "Chinese women are small ain't they? So are all these dresses tiny too?"

I roll my eyes. "Of course not, they make European sizes."

I hand him reimbursement for the stock to be delivered to his address.

He says "Cheers, Annie Jones."
I wince. Old school days chum. Far too familiar.

I fetch my exquisitely embroidered "Exclusive Designs By Anastasia" labels.

And start to unpack and do what I like to call Recasting.

My own labels are beautifully sewn in of course because I'm always, always The Professional.

7.
Painting by Words

Helen Connor

Along a single path, following a theme

The crossroads up ahead, painting a different scene

That way could be picnics, dancing and delight

That way could be demons, scarecrows that fright

A Narnia of wonders is just within my reach

If I only follow my pencil, who knows what it will

teach.

Photography © David Brand

8.
Tudor Tumult

J.E.Hall

—

A story in the context of cataclysmic events around
Ottery St Mary, July 1549

*First in a mornyng whan thou arte waken and purpose ryse,
lyfte up thy hande and bless the, and make a Synge of the holy cross, In
nomine patris et filly et sprites sancta, Amen…
And if thou say a pater noster, an Ave and a crede,
and remember thy maker, thou shalt spede moch the better.*

John Fitzherbert – The Boke of Husbandry (1533)

In the 3rd week of July 1549 Lord Russell is ordered to get
foot soldiers from Somerset and Dorset – *If they won't fight
against the 'rebels and papists of Devon' - they shall be deemed
traitors, forfeit their lands, homes, goods, wives and children without
hope of pardon.*

Eamon Duffy – Voices of Morebath p133

Anthology

The name's Bo, as in Bo Peep, sheep. Real name Robert
Yeo, sometimes Bob the shepherd. Got it?

Big trouble. I'm in the middle of it, on the front line.
No way out. It's as bad as it gets. An ongoing nightmare.
When men hate each other so much they see rats' eyes and
tails in one another. We are plague carriers, creatures fit only
for killing, and themselves, pure, precious as a gold coin and
loyal to the king whose head is on the coin. When people
see others as vermin, you know it's real bad. I've seen the
hard glint in their eyes, from the gold I guess, and then
there's nothing else for it, 'cept they want to purge you with
sharp metal and fire. As I say, it's a hell of a time.
Everyone's against everyone right now, or should I say
us ordinary folks, us commoners, are against the masters;
and masters are against the likes of us. The rich gentry
bubble like foam floating to the top in a barrel of ale. The
rest of us, like so much brown sediment sink to the bottom
waiting to be sluiced away as so much soil
water.
My grandad trapped rats, then he drowned them. He'd
search them out by our chickens every morning and then
he'd push them under the water with a forked stick. I
watched him. He knew what he was doing. He just got on
with it. I know killing when it's going on. Don't like it, but
it's chickens or rats isn't it, no more complicated than that?
There's us in the west, and the gentry and the kings men up
against us. I'll come on to that presently.
It's late in the day, well into July, maybe three weeks
in, the height of summer. Normally St James Day 'bout

now, – but all that's gone… We've all been ploughing, killing the weeds. Crops are showing signs of ripening, first hay's been cut. The trees are heavy with leaf, a darker shade of green, and the air smells of dry grass and wild flowers. However, Ottery minds are not on the land, no-one's thinking about the coming harvest, no, all the talk is about the rising in the west and the need to defend ourselves against the new false religion.

Vast numbers of good Devon men are on the move across the whole shire and word is they're heading our way, men on foot with pitchforks and bill hooks and bags of determination. We're rising up and thousands upon thousands I've heard are gathering on the north side of Exeter at St David's Down. Then there's the Cornish, thousands more fighting men coming to join us under Humphrey Arundell's leadership. Like an incoming tide, men are sweeping in, making their way north and east and into the River Otter Valley. Yeah, right here!

Last month, the Carew brothers, Peter and Garwen, two local governors, well known Otter Valley gentry and even better known now since everyone's moanin' about them, really stirred it. They acted so bad. Instead of meeting us, listening, hearing our grievances, they aggressively proceeded to fire the barns and then people's homes in Crediton. The knaves! Word is, it was Peter Carew pointing at the houses he wanted torched! They went further, topped those misdeeds having ten good people killed. All this just seven miles north of Exeter.

That's not all they've done neither! Mid-June trouble brewed over the Whitsun Festival the other side of Crediton, at Sampford Courtney. When the priest and good people there objected to the King's new prayer book they also got badly treated. Those Carews have played their part in causing panic across the west. We've had more than enough. Things have come to a head like a boil ripe to be lanced. Well, that was the trigger point, though we were already a much wronged and grumbling people.

Today, Exeter's already surrounded, cut off and has been under siege since the beginning of July. God's bones! What a bad decision – they've signed themselves up with the King's cause. Couldn't they see sense and fall in with Plymouth and all of us? What hurts me most about Exeter is how the cathedral under Dean Haynes has betrayed our faith for years – how that man is hated! He went about saying, "I'm cleansing the cathedral and city of the sin of idolatry". That was his way of abusing the old religion, the true faith, the way we all love.

Let me tell you more gossip I've heard. Other Ottery gentry have also betrayed us. I'll give you their names – John Bodley, John Prestwood and John Periam, yes them – three Ottery men, but also Exeter merchants. Well, once the siege of Exeter started, those three came over this way and told the King's military man in these parts Lord Russell, they'd help him raise troops! Knaves! He was all set to run away east, but they've been persuading him to resist the people. It's scandalous. I'd love to know where those three are hiding now?

Our peaceful little Otter Valley is changing. Battle lines are being drawn by the day. Russell, based in Honiton, maybe less than ten miles to the east wants to relieve Exeter before it falls or comes over to us. Put simply and starkly, that leaves Ottery where I am right now, and Alfington where I live, and all our neighbouring villages, caught where tinder strikes flint, right in the middle of an explosive conflict. As for us local people, all our sympathy is with the cause, but what can we simple folk do? Much as we support the Rising, we're caught between a rock and a hard place.

What happens to us now? All I know is Russell's army's been on the move today. You could hear them, several hundred men, half on horse. An army can't move silently. Earlier, soon after first light, they were seen skirting Ottery following the river, before trying to head for Exeter on the main road. This morning you could hear the sound of armour and horses and the ominous regular beat of military drums and marching feet. Tonight, angry, tired and frustrated they've come straight here into Ottery. Pretty well everyone's hidden inside their homes.

The place is crawling with both men on horse and foot soldiers, some of those from foreign parts with huge long swords, the height of a man. They'll want, they need a victory and I can tell they haven't got it. They wanted to free Exeter today from those who are besieging it and they haven't. Exeter's just over ten miles from here, normally a half day walk along a straight road and easy to reach, up and over the commons and down the other side – normally I say, 'cept now I know, because I helped, along with everyone else, the way's blocked, closed off to them, because over the past couple of days we felled every tree we could, giant oaks as well as holly and left them across the road, shutting it, rendering it impassible.

Even horses couldn't jump or find a way through what we did, let alone Russell's foot soldiers. Those poor people in Exeter, a bad business, they could soon one way or another be dead too, or not… if they had any sense, like I said, they'd switch sides. What'll they do? Hunger often makes a man's mind up for him… no-one knows. The whole world's gone mad. Everything's upside down. We could soon all be butcher's meat, so much red blood on Devon's red earth, waiting to be washed into our ditches and rivers.

Tonight there's going to be burning in Ottery. I can see small fires have been lit by the soldiers, surely a sign of what's to follow. I'm watching Russell's tired and frightened men, having given up getting to Exeter, knowing the whole county's against them, now turning on Ottery, just because they can. They pause in the Flexton, an open space in front of the church, where we have our weekly market. They linger, talking in short tempered bursts, arguing together with one another in malcontent, in angry plotting, with raised and furious tones.

It's decided. Then I see them rise, faces aglow. They split into small groups and start firing good Ottregian homes, all on Lord Russell's orders I guess. He's supposed to be here – somewhere. Word is he's shitting himself like sheep on wet field days. We think he's so frightened he could do anything. People say he just wants to run back to Honiton, but he'd rather run much further east, Dorset, Somerset even. He could be a loser and that's scary for him, would be for anyone. In times like this there's no safe sanctuary to be found. This isn't a bad place where I'm watching from – I can see what's going on.

I'm sitting in the grassy, unkempt Ottery churchyard; which no-one cares for any more. It's all overgrown with high grass and nettles and cow parsley. I'm sitting low, keeping my distance, leaning on a headstone watching the firing of the houses opposite; soldiers, like hungry feral dogs are walking hurriedly from house to house seeing what they can find, then holding out burning fire brands, teasing and laughing as they bother occupants and torch their precious homes. There's nothing I can do… 'cept watch…

They're swaggering in the arrogance of power, smiling, holding their orange flaming torches up against low hanging thatch waiting the seconds it takes to catch, which it does, all too easily, every time. In these dark days I've learned that death and destruction's a quick process. Creating hell takes just moments, believe me, I'm seeing it all. I'm watching it again right now. What's nearly as bad is that there's nothing, not a bloody thing I can do to stop them. No-one knows when they'll have had their fill.

I'm sitting still, keeping quiet, staying low, keeping out of the way. I don't want to draw attention to myself, it's my way of surviving. Learnt that a long time ago. As a shepherd lad, poorly dressed, small for my age, I've a life time of being picked on and pushed around. I'm carrying a four month old lamb under my arm. The last one, she escaped from the sale of one hundred assorted sheep, happened to have found herself a way out, so I picked her up. Finders keepers.

Just so you know about me and Lambkin; it's me trying to tell them I'm no soldier, trying to convince I just mind sheep, I'm only a lad, and I'm absolutely no threat. But whether they'll see me as not worth the bother – no-one knows, so I'm keeping my head down, my body still.

If they spot me, I can't be sure they'll swallow it. I'm poor, skinny, inconsequential, definitely no hero; I keep telling myself they won't be interested in me. I watch, I see what they do. I notice things, I remember things, I will remember it all. I always have. It's a gift I can memorise – even recall the old prayers we're not allowed to use. They can't see that. It's all my secret.

The wind shifts, there's a new tang to the warm summer air. I smell the job in hand – the acrid, smoking timber and thatch; I taste the bitter ash. I hear the crackling flames, the yells, squeal of pigs, barking of dogs, screams as families try to pull children out of harm.

I hear shrieks and the groaning of men on being roughed up, watch animals and whatever else hastily thrown out of homes as familiar faces gather powerlessly to watch helplessly as everything goes up in flames. I look on, watch still others throwing things from upper windows into the street hoping they won't smash their cribs, pails and tables into pieces; that something, however small, might be saved.

If I were braver I might go and help. I hope no-one knows I'm here, I feel my skin crawl anticipating the the accusations and recriminations to come later. I know everyone, that's the trouble with a village like Ottery. I'll have to face them when the time comes – if I live that long…

Suddenly it gets brighter as a gust of wind spins sparks high and yellow flames dance furiously in the darkening sky. I watch mesmerised, never seen anything like it. It's followed later by charred debris spilling down from above like Satan's sooty snow. It begins to leave a dark grey dusting on the beaten earth of Paternoster Row. The days of processions along this road, reciting the Lord's Prayer, to finish at Amen Corner have turned to ash. There is death in the air. I watch quietly, taking it all in, still as a gravestone, watching like a stalking cat.

1549's been such an angry year; these past weeks especially so. It's like a beehive's been kicked over, the bees go wild bringing trouble, getting angrier and angrier, everyone diving for cover, no-one knowing if it's their turn to get stung next. Disabling shock and hurt feelings are all around like a plague. The bees anger spilled east, took off in Devon and Cornwall to land in Ottery and the River Otter valley, sparks fly and flames blaze. Fate's made us the battle zone, where it'll all get decided, maybe…

Presently the West's up in arms against the king, with Exeter isolated, besieged this past month. Who can imagine how difficult that is? The boy King Edward's no more than Somerset's performing or is it reforming puppet? It's not Edward who upsets me, but the Duke of Somerset. Somerset's the one who rules supreme, we all know that. Somerset's King in all but name, and he's hated for it.

And it's Russell who's been sent to fight that fiery redhead Somerset's battles. Word is that Russell's scared and so he ought to be. These past weeks he's been trying to recruit local soldiers, but I'm telling you he can't get a single man worth calling a man to join him! What does that tell you? How's that for a measure of where true sympathy lies? That's if you don't count the gentry, people with big houses and money to protect. It's a foregone conclusion they'd all signed up as loyalists, they always have, since before time began. Them and us, I've mentioned that already, but there it is.

Why don't those in London leave us be? Things weren't so bad a few years back, until they began taking

everything from us, and I mean everything. You've no idea
how much we've been provoked, how much they've stolen.
I'm telling you, they robbed us all until there was nothing
left but a little bit of fight to try and make them stop.

I need to tell my tale because no-one else can. All are
too afeard. While I sit and watch these flames what else can
I do but reflect and reminisce? I hope you're listening
carefully. These flames are just the latest manifestation of
the destruction being wrought upon us.
Where to start? You attack a man's religion, you attack his
very soul and that's what's been happening here. Not just
once or twice, but time and time again. That's where the
root of it all lies in my humble opinion. Ask any Devonian
or Cornishman. We're a proud people and we won't be told
how we should practice our Christian Catholic faith. We're
free and want to stay free. Why has what we've always done
suddenly become treason.

Bear with me.. I need to go back three, four years, and
tell you what happened when I was a lad of eleven. I
remember 1545 so well; back in King Henry's time, though
by then he wasn't the fit man he used to be. It hadn't been
going well for Henry, had it? He needed money for his wars,
his court and God knows what else. No-one knows where
all that money he took went. He holds his money like a
sieve holds water – he just isn't made to do it. My friend
Peter, south field ploughman's made the same, a whole
weeks 5 pence spent on ale before Monday night.

Henry had fallen out with the Pope trying to get his
divorce from Catherine of Aragon, giving us yet more
problems. His Archbishop, Cranmer, levered crafty reforms;
so that everything we knew became tainted by his attacks on

our commoner's religion. We knew what direction the wind was blowing, we didn't like it, no-one did, but we couldn't do anything.

One time stands out. Was December 1545 worse for us in Ottery than what Russell's troops are doing today? Hard to say, the evidence isn't all in, no-one yet knows… but as I see it, these past three, four years have taken us into the very fires of hell.

Money! King Henry liked his lavish lifestyle, his run of wives, his fancy hunts, his wars. Can't tell which came first, probably the lavishness because he needed money, loads of it – but what do I know? Where did he get it from? I know the answer to that one – us, the ordinary people; but you're not allowed to say that – "'tis treason", my Mum always tells me.

She always calls me "wayward", her word for my thinking what I shouldn't. Sometimes I used to say what I shouldn't say too, but I'm wiser about that now and button my lip. "You were born the wrong side", my Mum says, and "that makes you a wrong'un. You'll never need to find trouble, it'll always will find you my lad!" Guess I'll always be "my lad" to her.

She also says most days presently, "Keep your mouth shut, mind yourself, forget it!" She's always saying that to me, means well, but she says it too often, like she says her rosary, it's become her creed. Even rosaries are something. You have to hide them now. I tell her, "'tis treason to have a rosary", but then how's she supposed to say her prayers? That's the only way she's ever known. Why doesn't Cranmer know that – common sense if you ask me…

41

She worries a lot, but then with good reason, the world's gone crazy and since Dad died she relies on me, her only one. I'm the church shepherd, the bread winner, well… I was the church shepherd, until all the sheep were sold off… and looking after Lambkin hardly qualifies me as being a shepherd, now does it? Who knows how we'll manage now? There just isn't any money and what there is won't buy enough.

Let me tell you about sheep, because that's what I really know. Since I was a boy, shepherding's been my thing, like my Dad before me, but it's also been the king's thing, because he's been rustling our sheep out of our possession since I was small. I'm not joking. In a sheep county, like Devon, he took a particular and spiteful aim at us, it was personal and he hit us hard. All men and lads have to go and practice archery, go down to Butts Lane to do it, so I know what taking aim at a target is about and Henry took aim at us, at our sheep. I mean, it was only at the start of lambing this year there he taxed our sheep. Listen here, tax starts at 3 pence on every ewe. Just think! A grown up shepherd only earns 5 pence a week, that's massive! Yes, I can hear your question, it was 3 pence on every sheep we had.

Somerset's Commissioners, his taxmen, have been round in a gang of three, one of them a bought-off priest in tow the whole time. Tax collectors – we know what the Bible thinks of them! They went round the whole of Devon I'm told, taxing every sheep they could count and what's more, if people didn't sell them quick enough they were done for. So many are bankrupt – livelihoods gone, and forced out of house and home. That's why I'm an ex-shepherd. You won't find any sympathy for loyal subjects round here! We've been fleeced! Sorry about that. And Lambkin, she's not got any friends but me.

Yes, Henry wanted money, loads of it, but worse, those round him, they wanted even more, to rob us of our very selves. Don't believe me? Well listen here, no-one else will have the guts to tell you. Taxes on sheep, lamb by lamb, taxes on wool pound by pound. Even the church bees have been taken! No-one can tell you when taxes were ever levied so high – that's because there never was a time so bad! But like I say, robbing men of money is one thing, stealing their faith and forcing them to take on another religion, that's another. Some say that's worse, but I wouldn't know. I'm a lad.

So that's what's been happening. What do you think of that? Since '45, everything round here's got sold off to pay bloody Henry! We're all starving paupers. Except, that is, what cunning people and of course the lofty aristocracy and well to do gentry squirrel away. We all know they still have meat on their tables, four meats for lunch is what I hear. All we get is bread and pease pottage if we're lucky.

And there's another thing that rancours. Henry's been debasing our currency for years, taking gold and silver coins and replacing them with base metal, copper if you were lucky. That's one more of his ways of robbin' the common people. Not that I've ever seen a gold coin, I might add. It's just what I've heard and as I keep saying, what do I know? All I see is no-one with money any more…

Henry started robbin' the monasteries, the priories, the churches ages ago, can't say when, well before my time. There's been a full frontal attack on our religion, our faith, our church and before long he'd turned his gaze on us, his greedy eyes fixing on Ottery and he thought, "Huh! I see more rich pickings". Not that any of that had ought to do with me. Money was so rare I was lucky to see a farthing let alone a halfpence, but he had his eye on our Ottery's prized assets and he said to himself, "they've got my name on them". Let me tell you what happened because no-one will tell you. Everyone's silenced by dread and terror. 'Tis true!

Back in the past, the one thing Ottery St Mary was noted for was its grand Collegiate Church; its fine buildings and magnificent two lofty bell towers; and its ever whistling weather cock – the pinnacle of the church builders work, a bird without pity, keeps us all awake with its incessant blasting noise, even whenever there's the slightest breeze. Come a strong wind, you can hardly think for the noise. He never lets up in trying to get us down, so I've started calling him Cocky Henry! There must be some church cock maker laughing his head off in heaven at the centuries of misfortune his bird's inflicted on generations of Ottregians. Trouble is that cock's so high and out of reach there's no stopping it. No-one knows how to kill a noisy cock. And how do you stop a Henry or a Somerset for that matter?

Two centuries ago, maybe more, Bishop Grandisson built this monumental church to mimic his cathedral in Exeter. My… it's fine and splendid. and back then no expense was spared to give us something really good. Proudly stands in gleaming white Beer Quarry stone. Look at it, behind me, over my shoulder, a church on a hill, a light shining above the river and the village. Look at the sunset behind setting it off, a real picture; a seat of learning; some say Devon's answer to Oxford and Cambridge, but I wouldn't know about that.

Writers of Ottery

What a place this was back then. So many lived and worked for the church – clergy, laity and the businesses of Ottery thrived on, depended on it. The choir, all the priests, and talking of learning, we're so proud of our Alexander Barclay. Yes, he's a very old man now I'll grant you, but his book, 'Ship of Fools' still amuses us. Showed the church clergy to be as debauched, ordinary, and as open to the vices common to man as the next person. We all knew it and Alexander told it how it was, truly a man of the people!

Perhaps the day will come again when we can all tell it how is without being told we're committing treason. There's power in telling it straight. Too often truth is what we're told it is, not that secret thing what we know it to be.

We love all the characters that made our village. But these past few years, since '45, what once was vibrant colour has latterly become but grey shadows. Our lifeblood's been leached from us and I fear things will get worse, it's so bad it's taking the very heart out of the place.

Good grief! My God! Look! Yellow flames are bursting high in the darkening sky, twice the height of that house. Thank God the wind's from the south west or the church and the rest of the settlement will go up too. Those burning cottages in Silver Street and Sandal Street are sending bright sparks high in the sky. Can't tell where else is burning, possible over on the Ridgeway, but I can't see from here. It's such a hot summer's evening, everything's tinder dry. The whole place could go up and then we'd be entirely finished.

The minutes pass. I'm watching scurrying men about their criminal business. My guess is half are foreign, mercenaries, paid soldiers, men of grunts and swords, with no mercy. Not for long though. Look! Those soldiers are being called off by a bearded man in charge, him with the brandished sword, swinging round and round, glancing this way and that frightened he'll miss something, the guy on a surly brown horse, a horse with a weepy eye. Could it be Russell himself? "Your job's done!" he's shouting. He's desperately waving them on, shooing, swinging his horse round in tight circles, wanting to get them away. I know a scared man when I see one.

They're moving up North Street, making for safety. But two of those arsonist infantrymen are so enjoying their task they want to carry on. Scoundrels! How can you want to burn down people's homes? Burning, flames, chaos, destruction inflicted on ordinary commoners. Ah ha! they're coming away now. Orders are orders I guess. All are strangers, not from round here, they've no doubt got their own reasons for taking the king's blood money.

Where was I? Well, until 1544, our Warden of the College, long-suffering John Fyssher, ran things round here. But then Henry, greedy, grasping Henry, needing yet more money saw our college and church as so much scrappage, precious metals and quality cloths all his for the taking. Dissolution it was called. I'd never heard the word before. Rape or murder, robbery too, I call it.

Henry's inventory writing ruffians, his fat tellers, his greasy accountants with grasping claws and penning fingers – they drained the valley's lifeblood, line by line, item by item. Together they brought everything that had been our tradition, the world we knew, to an end. Killed this place, bled it dry. It was riches to rags for all common people. Centuries of good, that's if you forget for a moment the Black Death that killed half the folk; centuries of good

religion, good living, when everyone knew their place – it
was all just taken away.

Yep, by the end of '45, Henry's men had destroyed Ottery.
It's treason to say so, but hear this – I BLAME HIM. Like
some robbing Barbary pirate, Henry looted all our treasures
and sacked our communities. Look around here on any
market day these days, every head round this place is
stooped in sadness, good people felled into dire poverty, no
religion to fall back on. Everyone left heaving with
resentment; yes, all that and more…

Other good people have left us, those landless,
jobless, homeless sods; gone to live with family or friends
elsewhere, anyone who could have them. Whoever heard of
refugees in our own valley before? Not me! Thereafter, after
dissolving the church, dissolution-ing it, if that's the word,
there was no singing, no bell ringing, nothing – just a silent
vacuum where once there'd been life. All the employment,
all the processions, all the saints days, colourful festivals, all
the lights, all the wealth, all the jobs – gone, for the King
said he had need of it. "Huh!"

There's the thing. I grew up thinking soldiers were to
defend us…. That was before…

"Hell!" That soldier's seen me. He's coming my way.
No way out, nowhere to run. Time to look innocent. What
does he want? "Lambkin, come closer, look who's coming."

I stand awkwardly, raising myself slowly, not wanting
to look tall, one hand half lifted in innocent greeting, the
other still clutching Lambkin tight to my chest. I try a goofy
smile. It doesn't seem to work, he draws his sword. My
heart is racing, my mouth drops open.

"It's only me, Shepherd Bo, watching the fires…" I plead. I don't know whether he's listening or heard me and my voice sounds childlike, pathetic.

He's right up close, too close, towering over me, smells of smoke and unwashed soldiering, wet sweat marks staining his grey shirt, black smears across his nose, his hairy cheeks and heavy brow. A savage face with tired, black rimmed eyes. He draws his sword drawn, raises it up, shoulder high. With his other hand he's reaching out, for me… but grabs Lambkin round the neck and roughly pulls, snatches him from my grasp. I don't resist, and he smirks as I stagger back and fall, my back against a grave. Will he leave me dead… it's a fitting place?

He pauses, raises his sword above me. My head drops, I don't breathe or dare move. I sense him bending lower and then growling he whispers in my ear with a snigger and a London accent, "Thanks for supper, Bo," before turning, running with his now bleating prize, chasing after his waiting mate up ahead to tell him of his unexpected bounty. Then they're gone, all the soldiers following the man on the horse, Lambkin too.

Breathing deeply, relief washing over, I see the tail end of them gathering, to retreat in some kind of order, finally disappearing round the corner into Paternoster Row, heading north in the direction of Alfington and their base camp of two weeks near Honiton. Someone's begun tapping out a regular drumbeat as they fall in line.

I don't feel I need to hide any more and cautiously look on at the devastation around me. I could see they were unpredictable, frightened and frustrated men just waiting to take it out on us because of what had happened earlier in the day. This morning they'd followed the river, skirting Ottery, only to find their progress to relieve Exeter blocked. They knew it was us, the common people of Devon rising against them, that'd done it. They were spot on, of course we did it! Adding to their sense of frustration, they'd failed to engage any meaningful enemy force; just small skirmishes had occurred here and there, was all I'd heard, but nothing decisive. The Rising was still a growing threat for them. They've gone for now, but like lice, they'll be back. Our adversaries won't ever leave us in peace. The King, sorry, Dooky Somerset, won't allow it.

Apart from the roars and hisses of still burning straw and timber, there's nothing but the occasional wail from women on the warm breeze. Darkness is beginning to fall. On July nights like this, the reality of darkness comes slowly, night steals upon you as the day keeps hanging on, like a lover, reluctant to leave its beloved.

More loss to bear, and apart from life itself, what is still left for us? Sometimes I think futility and hopelessness are as deadly an enemy as soldiers. Only those away from the front line can have the luxury of dreaming of victory. Make no mistake, Ottery and our neighbouring settlements are on the front line in this war, and being here means no-one knows which way all this will turn out.

I turn my gaze away from the smouldering ruins to spy the houses of the wealthy. Unsurprisingly they've been left untouched. To be sure, this was an attack on us commoners, ordinary folk. The powerful punishing the powerless, seeking to cause us fear and dread – not hard to do. Life's become all about us and them when once we rubbed shoulders and kind of got along most of the time.

Anthology

I've recently learned it's the time to shut up, the time for non-conversations, a time for silence, when having only underground private thoughts is safe. It stands to reason. The use of open words, careless talk, simply paves the way to more suffering and death. And I mean really suffering, inflicted by the experts in pain, those practiced and equipped in their dark art and their Tudor masters, their paymasters; those who until only a couple of years ago happily used boiling to death as a means of execution. Cruel times demand careful use of words.

I'm not sentimental about sheep. Life's too hard for that. Lambkin was going to one pot or another. Better Lambkin taken than me. I'll need to go foraging now all the lambs are gone. Not my favourite, but peas, beans and roots boiled up will have to do. Now Russell's troops have all gone for the night, there'll be no more action, unless... unless they lay waste to Alfington on their way back. Alfington folks, like Ottery folks sent men to the fight. They too could face a firing, or worse. I need to get home and so you know, I'm an Alfington lad, that village is, and always has been, my first home.

I'm telling you this as I get up from my grassy graveyard eyrie and carefully begin my walk home, keeping a watchful eye out for stray soldiers. Adjacent to the dark church, I pass the derelict stone buildings of the ruined College and make my way past the empty Warden's House. It looks like an abandoned builders yard, stones everywhere. Stones that people help themselves too! I'll tell you more presently.

I'm taking the back way home, safest down beside the River Otter, avoids meeting those soldiers again who'll be on the road. I'm thinking they'll be tired, scared, wanting to take the quickest route back to their HQ. This way's usually a slow, muddy overgrown track, though dry now as it's midsummer. The path runs north and west of Ottery, beside riverside apple orchards and fields, straight back to our cottage on the north western edge of Alfington, maybe not fifteen minutes away.

A sudden panic, a sense of dread stops me in my tracks. Will Mum be OK, will our home be spared, will…? I must move on and faster. Running, I dodge low branches in the increasing gloom and curse whenever one I miss smites me across my face. A pair of owls make early calls to each other with their tu-whit tu-woos sing song, which feels all out of place, as if nature is out of step with reality; wise owls should know and respect this time of human suffering. No-one is sure of things any more; some are saying even the earth is no longer the centre of the universe but the sun is. I feel all is now disorder.

I mentioned the stones by the church earlier. You might think with shepherding at an end I'd be a begging vagrant too; some might say I'm one of the luckier ones. I get work sometimes at John Haydon's Cadhay Manor. For those who don't know Ottery, Cadhay's one of the three under-manors. With the dissolution in '45 Somerset took the main Ottery Manor, the one by the church with all the land. How come?– a just man might ask. I can't answer.

Yet so far as I know, Somerset's never been there, let alone lived there. He's got his own fine place in London from what I hear. Word is, he demolished the church of St Mary, in the Strand, to build his own stately pile – a fine, top dog, city mansion no less. I'm surprised he stopped at that. I imagine it's probably a palace in all but name! I heard in the ale house, some poor London labouring lads like me were paid to carry the stones from St Paul's Cathedral to build it, yeah! I believe it. Somerset also took the cathedral wainscotting from St Paul's I hear; so when you hear that kind of detail, well, it's got to be true, hasn't it? Same's happened here, gentry help themselves, think they're entitled, though a few stones have gone into other houses, one along the Ridgeway… Henry and all his thieves, I hate the lot of them.

What I'm telling you is – this is what they euphemistically call the reforming dissolution, but it's probably not the message you hear from the powers that be. You know what I mean, the system that lets the rich tell the story and take their pickings. It all means Dooky Somerset and his friends can all live like kings.

It's commonly held that the First Duke of Somerset and God knows where else, is truly the King of England in all but name… that's the gospel truth, that's the reality, I've made it clear already, but I'm telling you again in case the penny hasn't dropped. Loyal subjects, and you might be one, don't like to believe these thing are true, now do they? Think about it. I'd swear to it on the Pope and Blessed Virgin's name…

Like I say, think about it. What can that small eleven year old kid King Edward, two years younger than me, know about ruling, know about anything for that matter? Nought! The world is really run by Somerset and his men.

Somerset might be Lord of the Manor but he doesn't show his face round here. He's always been an absentee landlord. For all I know he's happy just taking Ottery's money. His stooge Lord Russell's his man of the moment, sent down here from London to knock us in the west into shape. Keep the peasant buggers down…

As I was saying, well beginning to explain, Ottery Manor is the main manor, but Cadhay, Knightstone and Holcombe are the under-manors. These three places all have their own gentry in charge, but for me, Cadhay's been the place for me to make some money.

I have to confess I'm ashamed of what I do, though proper confession to a priest is hard to make these days; but I only do exactly what John Haydon tells me. Yes, I filch those very stones from the church's old college buildings – stones from its library, cloisters, chapter house, any good building stones I can chip off and make away with, anything I can take from the many buildings that have been forced to close. There's so much there, I think I'll be busy for years… maybe…

All I do is take and clean the stones, and with Geoff's help I take them all with him in his cart to Cadhay. There we unload them for the stonemason to use. Whilst we all struggle and get poorer by the day, he and the gentry get richer. John Haydon wants those stones to build himself a fine new Cadhay Manor House. Oh, I get paid by the cart load, works out three pence a week. Perhaps he and Somerset share plans? I wouldn't know, but he has to get his lofty ideas from somewhere. I like the Bible story, the one Jesus told of the rich man who builds ever bigger barns… you know the one, where the rich man gets his comeuppance. It's become one of my favourites. I think there's a judgement and we reap whatever we sow.

I've done a few trips now and the money's enough for me and Mum. Guy, the steward who runs Cadhay house for John Haydon says, his Master, being a lawyer, has been much used by Henry to carry out the dissolution orders and then by Somerset to continue closing priories and religious houses all over Devon. We all know that man Haydon's done well out of it, like his fellow criminal Somerset. No-one locally dares cross him, he's untouchable, he get first pickings from the spoils left by the king. Like, he's the local governor round here. What I mean is, he's the king's man on the spot, and well, he's Somerset's man isn't he? First he had Henry's ear, now he has Edward's. That's how it is. The rich get richer, and me, I just move stones.

What choice do I have to do any different? There's no other job. I don't like what I do. Every cartload is a hollow reward. With every stone taken off site, it's like taking the soul from the church. All the choristers, clergy, trainee priests, chantry intercessors, sacristan, vergers, bell ringers, cooks, candle makers, librarian, clerks, maybe forty or more people, I never counted, all gone too. When will it stop? What'll be left of Bishop Grandisson's gift to this place? Will the fine old church building itself be next in line for the chop? Who knows? It's already a shadow of what it was and there's no-one caring for it.

Huh! That reminds me, in the vacant space since the position of Warden was dissolved, the church has been left neglected, the income it once had all gone. Under the King's say so, Haydon's been made one of four so-called Governors to run what's left of the church. That's a laugh. Already townsfolk are taking a case to court for his abject neglect in his duties as Governor. My guess is, he'd be quite happy to get the very best remaining stones from the church building itself and create an even bigger, grander Cadhay Manor. But what do I know? We'll have to wait and see. Maybe he'll keep the church for his own fine memorial chapel? No-one says mass for souls or lights candles any more. So who knows what will happen? Who knows?

Alfington! Nearly there, best be careful, make a slow approach. There's a noise, a murmuring on the night breeze. The soldiers must have stopped up as they were passing by. Some disturbance is under way. It's in the air, the sounds of night are all wrong. Alfington's under attack. Definitely time to lie low. I've already had one scare too many. I can't be invisible much as I wish it, for there's still a hint of light in the clear summer night sky. The moon and stars are already providing more light to see by for mischief-making in the shadows. As I get nearer I hear yells, shouts and screams and crouch down. I think it's over to my right hand side on the east side of the village, nearest to the through road from Ottery to Honiton.

I'm imagine Russell's soldiers moving from cottage to cottage in Alfington, beating, abusing, thieving… These are my neighbours, my friends. I hear more cries. These heart rending yells continue… How long? I want to stop my ears but can't…

After a while, just as in Ottery earlier, there's a worrying silence followed by a sudden firing of houses, maybe just those nearest the road. Looks like several homes have been fired. Maybe Mum is safe. She always listens out and hopefully she heard what was coming and escaped toward the river, hiding amongst the oaks and holly trees along its steep bank. The isolation of our tiny cottage on the outskirts might save her and our home.

Another half an hour has passed and I'm think the soldiers have had their sport and are moving off again toward their camp. They haven't stopped long. It's time for me to begin approaching home. On the one hand the advantage is all mine, these paths, these hedges, these trees are all my playground and I know all the hiding places and how to best disappear. But on the other hand even that offers little comfort, tonight every dark corner feels hostile and I am easily afraid. I'm reminded of once, when I was naughty as a small child, I ran out into the night, hid outside the house to escape a beating. The same anguished feeling of fear lies there in the pit of my stomach.

So I pause and watch our tiny cottage from afar tucked in low by the Warren Field hedge before creeping slowly toward the wooden front door. I'm casting glances in every direction, and nowhere feels safe. I'm right upon her before I make her out, she's totally still and silent. I spot her before she hears or sees me. Now I see she's sitting all hunched up under the apple tree, looking scared, her face fixed upon our tiny home. Startled at my final approach, she soon realises who it is and moves quickly to seize and embrace me in pulsating emotion, flowing tears and gasping sobs.

"Bo? You're alive," she murmurs, "alive. My Bo…" and holds my face tenderly in her rough hands.

"But Lambkin's gone and we won't be getting him back… Don't suppose the soldiers came up as far as here?…"

"No, I heard them the other end of the village, I watched from the orchard. Someone called those dogs off, I heard them, they're rightly worried about rebels. For soldiers, they sounded very frightened, worried about obstacles in the road, getting ambushed at night. They've gone, I'm certain of it, but I fear some of our neighbours have fared badly... come on, let's go and see what we can do... but be careful and mind what you say..."

Arm in arm slowly and silently we wander up the dirt track toward our nearest neighbours and then on to the houses nearest the road. Once more I smell bitter smoke, it stings my eyes and hear the crackle of embers. I spot Jack, my best friend, sitting on the ground opposite what was once his home. He half smiles in greeting and shrugs in despair.

"Bo! It can be rebuilt. It would be worse if it had happened in winter," he adds, always the one to see a brighter side, but quite unable to hide the streaks tears had made on his ash stained cheeks. He waves his arm toward the side of the track, unable to speak. Two men lie there, in dark pools of blood, all too visible in the gloom. I can just make them out, two good men, Joseph and William, friends. Both worked the same fields all their lives often side by side together, Joseph the whistler and William the singer, now dying together. I picture them both in happier times....

"Come and stay with us tonight," I offer. "Bring Mary and your Mum and Dad," I tell Jack. He nods and gets up, heading out down the lane to find them.

"There's bread and pottage," Mum calls after.

He turns and adds, "The soldiers killed any man who looked useful, anyone they thought might be a rebel soldier.

They knew we'd helped in the rising. It was to be expected I suppose. Someone must have spilled the beans though, betrayed us, grassed us up... We're on the leading-edge here. Everywhere west of where we are is held by those defending the way we choose to do things. Have you heard how passionately those Cornishmen are in defending their traditions? I hear they've come with Arundell leading them, and have already reached Exeter to reinforce our Devon men. They've marched non-stop east for days to get here. Like us, they've had enough of being told how they must worship God and what language to use. Mind you half the time I can't tell what them Cornish are saying, but why shouldn't they do things the way they always have, the way they understand things. If it was alright in Henry's day, it 's still alright now by my reckoning, but don't tell anyone I say so..." Then he's gone.

"Mum, however this turns out, we've got to find a way for those in power to remember that we the commoners carry the cause of truth. There must be a way we can burn our own bright lights on dark nights, to show we rule our streets not them. They try to snuff us out like candles. Can't we light and hold a new flame and send them packing?

Tomorrow, I'm going to take Jack with me with any other lads I can find. We'll walk over to the rallying point in Feniton to join the fight. The word is, that's where the Rising will take its stand. After what I've seen I know it's time to stand and fight for all we hold dear.

One day, when things settle, when the Rising's done and the soldiers have all gone, when the history writers have made up their own story of what happened for everyone to believe; then us lads will meet again in the Ottery Ale Houses and we'll find a way to show the truth of it all, you wait! We'll roll a flaming barrel."

"Bo! You and your big ideas!"

Photography © Graham Bishop

9.
Banana Slices

Cynthea Gregory

Rodriguez cut the motor. We all peered ahead as the boat slid towards the over-hanging tropical vegetation.

Within seconds, the drone of the outboard was replaced by squealing, chirping, screeching. Shrill bursts echoed through the mass of greenness enveloping the runabout boat. Branches, leaves shook. One by one, we tourists, all in cumbersome life-vests, attempted to stand, folding almost in half, to gawp beneath the boat's canopy at the live theatre. The rainforest became alive with monkey chaos: elasticated limbs, clinging tails, inquisitive glances. Capuchins splattered a myriad greens. Monkeys and tourists scrutinised each other. Capuchin big, black gobstopper eyes and tight little mouths set in pallid faces, performed for our clicking phones and cameras.

"Oh, aren't they cute?" sang one American voice. Rodriguez, our guide, signalled for quiet—a finger to his lips. Then his horizontal hands told us all to sit. He set the example. Uncharacteristically, we all obeyed.

The throbbing of an enormous container vessel momentarily caught my attention, as it cut through Lake Gatan, heading for the next section of the Panama Canal. But the trembling trees held more interest, more excitement. In seconds though, the ship's wake beat against our boat, reminding us of its passage. We seesawed like a tiny boat on choppy seas; the water splosh, sploshing against the wooden framework.

Fruit appeared from nowhere. Tiny bunches of grapes and banana slices were passed around to each of the small group.

"Place it in the palm of your hand," Rodriquez instructed, "and-do-not-try-to-hold-the-monkeys!"
I cupped the fruit in my clammy hand: surveyed the already discolouring banana, the powdery bloom of the grapes. I weighed up our expectant performers. And we waited— human and monkey creatures.

"Quarrr, quarr …" rang through the air. It was Rodriguez's signal, emulating their call. The cue. 'Go monkeys go.'

Black and white fur descended. The bravest flashed to the outstretched hands. A few hesitated on the boat's rounded edge. Long nails clicked along the boat's structure. Rodriguez had a monkey on his arm; furry haunches perched fleetingly in the seats' gaps. The American shrieked as a forward capuchin sat on her shoulder.

My bare knees felt leathery, spiky feet. Delicate thin black fingers scooped up the banana—discarding the skins haphazardly. Nom, nom, nom—the snack was gobbled down. Soft fur brushed against my skin. I noted the neat black cap on my diner's head, wrinkled pink-splodged face, sharp, stained teeth.

As anticipated, I was completely ignored, but the creature was imprinting an indelible image on my mind—a treasure to hold for always.
In seconds, the fruit had disappeared, and then, so did the monkeys—back to their treetop homes, awaiting their next delivery of goodies. Quarrr, quarr.

10.
River Of Thoughts

Melanie Barrow

A trickle barely seen,
A thought germinating,
Winding away from the source,
Meandering an unknown course.
Gathering momentum, then
Depositions fall from the pen.
The river flows content
Until around a weir it's sent.
Round and round so turbulent,
Concentric circles to circumvent.
Then whoosh and on it goes,
Words gush, stories compose,
Thoughts crash against the mind.
Possibilities widen, unconfined,
And leave the consciousness -
Explode into spaciousness.

11.
Bangers and Mash

Simon Cornish

Imagine if you will, you are still a child. Usually when you get home from school, one or the other of your parents makes you a nice hot meal. Bangers and mash is your favourite. But today is different.

You sit down to eat and today you are waited on by Maurice. This is novel and you stare at him a moment while he twists his thin moustache into a sideways question mark. You hear the sound of chopping from the kitchen and look past the waiter and through the open door to see a large sweaty bald guy in a grimy vest preparing something with the aid of a large meat cleaver. With each chop, shock waves shudder from his arm, up through through the smooth broad mound of his shoulder to be absorbed by the rolls of fat at the back of his neck. He stops briefly as if aware of your scrutiny and turns his head slightly. Maurice gives an over emphasized 'ahem' and explains that your parents no longer want to cook and have sold the operation.

You are hungry and this smacks of metaphor, so you go along with it.

With his eyebrows almost in his hairline, Maurice offers you a bewildering array of dishes, but you honestly just want bangers and mash, so you ask him for that. With his mouth now a tiny dot beneath the expressive moustache he turns and strides into the kitchen where the chopping sounds have resumed.

When your meal arrives, not only is it shepherd's pie, but you also notice it is only about a third of the portion you would normally get from your parents. You query Maurice about the small portion size, he explains that he had to deduct a third to deliver it to your table and the chef had to take another third to prepare it. Annoyed, you tell the waiter that this is unacceptable and demand you get your meal from someone else. Maurice, his face now contorted into a punctilious exclamation mark, scuttles off.

After a few moments another waiter appears. One who looks suspiciously like Maurice but with dark sunglasses and a wig. This new waiter claims he is called Gary. Gary, rubbing the side of his long nose, claim he can offer a much better deal than Maurice, because this new deal now includes... he pauses for dramatic effect ...*a drink*.

Normally you can get your own drinks. With a frown you glance at heavyset chef clattering about in the now smoky kitchen. Once again he stops, caught in profile, his sloping brow sinking so low over his eyes it makes it impossible to tell if he's looking back at you. Swallowing, you turn your attention back to Gary and agree to the meal and drink that is being offered.

After a few minutes, with more crashing and smoke emanating from the kitchen, Gary brings you out a plate of liver and onions as well as *the drink*. It still looks like you are only getting a third of a meal and, you notice, a third of a glass of squash.

When you ask Gary about this, he patiently explains that you are getting a better deal than with Maurice. He informs you, glancing about as if to check for eavesdroppers then leaning in close, that you are actually getting thirty-four percent on both your plate and in your glass, and he and the chef are only taking thirty-three percent each. He wiggles his eyebrows suggestively.

You almost accept it, then, with a frown, call to Gary and ask for someone who can serve you a proper meal. Gary scuttles off.

After what seems ages, a commotion can be heard in the kitchen and a mariachi band strikes up a tune and steps through the doorway. They stand around you and, through the medium of song, explain to you that, once again, you are being offered a meal and drink deal. They strike a dramatic chord and the song ends.

As you continue to stare in confusion. The band starts another tune. The mariachi singer, who looks ever so slightly like Maurice with a gold tooth, a luxuriant false moustache, and wearing a sombrero, warbles that if you agree to have your meal and drink at this restaurant every night for the next week, they will give you an amazing introductory offer.

You ask about the offer and the band hits a wild crescendo of trumpets and guitars as the singer explains you will receive a fifty percent portion, while the chef and the waiter will only get a mere twenty-five percent each. He then sings some more words so fast you can't quite catch them. Something about offeronlyapplying-blah-blah-blah, but the mariachi music is very good and you are really really hungry at this stage, so you agree.

A short time later the mariachi singer comes out and serves your half meal. At least, this time it is bangers and mash. You tuck in accompanied by the sound of mariachi music. The bangers and mash tastes like bangers and mash, the squash is just squash.

The next night you come in from school for your dinner. The mariachi band has disappeared and today you only receive a quarter portion. It looks a bit like meatloaf. He introduces himself as Alphonse, though again, he looks suspiciously like Maurice but wearing a large false nose. He seems to have dispensed with moustaches entirely this time.

Surely there's been a mistake? You had a deal after all. Ah, Alphonse explains, but that was an introductory offer. As detailed in their terms and conditions. Now you have had one meal with them you are no longer a new customer. But this is even less than you would have got without the deal, you shout at him. The waiter points out that under the agreed deal, you not only have to pay the chef and himself, but also the mariachi band who sold you the contract in the first place.

And you get the same the next night and the next, and so on. stuck with having to eat the same food at the same table, cooked by the same terrifying chef, with an endless round of waiters you never asked for. None of them seem to be getting any thinner, while your portions of portions shrink with each round of deals.

Then you remember the good old days of last week when your parents used to cook bangers and mash.

12.
The Moroccan Connection

Prologue

Graham Bishop

Rabat, Morocco, July

Maria Velázquez was transfixed by the opulence of her surroundings in the royal palace of Rabat. To be within touching distance of two kings, Juan Carlos of Spain and Mohammed VI of Morocco, was an experience she had never expected to have when she started her work for the library in the monastery of the Escorial outside Madrid.

The ceremony was for the presentation to the King of Morocco of microfilm copies of hundreds of Arabic manuscripts originally belonging to the then Sultan of Morocco. Forced to flee to France in 1612 by a revolt against his rule, his library and belongings were loaded onto a French ship for the voyage. The ship was captured on the high seas by the Royal Spanish Navy and ever since his library had been in Spanish hands.

Maria's presence there was thanks to the invitation her boss offered his new young assistant a few days before. Señor José Gijón, director of the Library Security, told her his deputy had cancelled at the very last moment; would she like to accompany him in his place?

She had only been in her new post for a few weeks and an unworthy thought occurred to her as Gijón made his offer: would she be expected to do something for him in return? No, he wasn't like that. Or was he? There was something of the night about him, but so far, all good.

As she watched the proceedings, taking delight in every detail, she wondered why the ceremony was not in reverse. 'Shouldn't it be Spain which keeps the copies, Morocco which should regain the originals? But that's not how it is. This is just gesture politics.'

She was very aware that if she wished to keep her new job, she must never voice such an opinion in Señor Gijón's hearing.

***

If you would like to read more of The Moroccan Connection please go to my website www.vidocqpress.com

13.
Homeless

Helen Connor

Where am I now?
Psychedelic mural smells of urine
Ripped sleeping bag
In the doorway with dreaming dog

Where am I now?
Feeling hungry and needing a wee
The dog nuzzles, echoes the whine
Rushing footsteps and smells of coffee

Where am I now?
And why am I here?
Invisible life, pain that's not seen
Broken threads of love before

Where am I now?
Where am I going?
If I'm not here tomorrow
Will anyone care.......?

14.
My Safe Place

Bella Tiley, Prize Winner

This is my place. Confined. Confronting. Yet mine.

For as long as I can remember, I have been patrolling these corridors, searching, scrutinising for a subtle change, a chance for the infinite twisting corridors to end. Robust brick walls loomed over my every turn, yet this was comforting, homely.

I am the ghost. The ghost of the castle. Darkness is where I belong. Gliding silently over the paving, mist meeting with granite. I know these tunnels like the back of my hand (not that I can see it) and I will always belong here, for ever more and beyond. Or so I thought.

Hissing taunts at the deer heads on the walls, rasping orders at the rusty suits of armour. Juggling the bullets in the cabinet, whispering to my shadowy friends, I am the ruler of my prison.

Unknown and insignificant, I make use of my lowly life; marvelling at the banshees, and wishing their honour were mine. I snigger at the poltergeists, admiring their common heists, and whisk hurriedly after the orbs, their fun, I soak up and absorb.

All was peaceful and safe: the occasional skeletons waltzing past, the ghost children giggling as they raced to be first in line.

Then one day, everything changed. Sunlight slapped us all in the face with the force of a tsunami as the large oak doors that had been sealed for so long, swung open. Spirits who had been directly in front of the doors, including the choir of beautiful banshee, withered before my eyes and dropped to the ground, letting out terrible shrieks of pain and despair. Skeletons, ghosts, vampires and shadow fiends began fleeing for their lives, sobbing and begging, shepherding their infants towards cupboards and trapdoors.

I am no longer trapped, but freedom isn't always a good thing.

15.
Saturday Blues
(A football fan's lament)

Carl Gilleard

Another match ends in a heavy defeat
Shattered illusions abound
With heads bowed low, crestfallen fans shuffle out of the
ground
Who takes the blame? Referee, players, the management
team?
Who should atone for wrecking the dream?
For such an inept lacklustre display
For the faithful few who watch every game.

As the crowd disperse, no longer a throng
The discourse focuses on what went wrong
There's anger, frustration, a sense of despair
The consensus being the club doesn't care.
Everyone has an opinion but at the end of the day
The away team won much to the home fans' dismay
Yet again. A crying shame.

Hard earned money spent once more
On purchasing tickets for at best a boring draw
Why do they do it, week after week?
A heavy cross to bear for the meek and the weak
Steadfastly loyal to their home-town pride
Refusing to switch allegiance to a more fashionable side

Anthology

A betrayal of a kind that no true fan could abide.

One fan returns home after the game
Dejected, deflated, emotionally drained
His family recognise the all too familiar signs
'Lost again dad? Why do you bother
It's not as if it's a question of honour'.
Whatever the weather it's always the same
Leaving in hope returning in pain.

Deliberating whether to respond to the tease
He thinks better of it for they cannot conceive
It's a drug once taken you must constantly feed.
He seeks solace by browsing the on-line chatter
And finds the manager's post-match patter
'The lads worked hard and were unlucky today" he claims
Heavens above! Was he at the same game?

A few hours later and lying abed
All manner of thoughts run through his head
Should he take up fishing or golf instead
  Of supporting a team that gives little back to the dedicated
                                                            fan
Who understands that whatever the manager's game plan
However abysmal the last performance.
The following week he'll be there for the next instalment.

16.
The Folk Club

James Armstrong

Gas-fitter, shop assistant; housewife with time-idle palms;
enthused student, ambitious civil servant, teacher of infants,
bookmaker, roofer, all dressed as if just come from work.
Oh my! Why do you low down, devious musicians always
arrive in disguise; looking like us, the audience – normal?
We've long since twigged your subterfuge: you're nothing
but magicians.

But, there's this giveaway: that distinct eye-look: intense –
inward-drawn, far-away – harking for a clever tune slide:
minor into major, sharp chord changes; ears alert for
Myxolidian shifting to Dorian.

In this innocent pub, you're all deceitfully attuned to a secret
language passing by unlearned ears. It's padding across the
pale, herring-bone parquet, creeping round the intricate,
cabriole legs, sidling over glistening wood-grained table-
tops. Our drinks tremble in their tumblers.

Then it declares itself: a familiar folk tune: Geordie, Cajun,
Klezmer, Gaelic; from Abruzzo or The Appalachians. For
some serene minutes our minds are cleansed of this day's
labours. We push aside long-lived anxieties to bask, by
proxy, in tropes of countless lost-loves, other's heart-wrung
griefs. We indulge warm nostalgias; yet, too, enjoy unstinted

aural pleasure: bright, true and abundant as a robin's song. We're invited to inhabit this sound-space carved out of space. I recall Orpheus, whose playing charmed trees, beasts, even stones and intoned rivers to cease; I ask, 'Can I stay forever here?' We relish what a tune once meant; means this refreshed instant of virgin sounding. You dissemblers! Zealously minting new nostalgias; anointing us with startling dove-flies-from-trickster's-sleeve sensations.

Like spies, your lies lie concealed. Good manners hide your minstrelsy. Not a bare-faced one of you has a stave of coded cyphers before you! Your fingerprints must be centuries-old nests of finely-held melodies.

You: player disguised as accordionist, with effrontery, flit to violin as natural as scratching your own head! Another, feigning to be a mandolin player, adopts the flute as if cooing a lullaby to her infant child. From bowing to blowing, pressing to plucking! Promiscuous charlatans, the lot of you! The cheek of it! Your subterfuge is in full view! Is there no rule that trims your philandering, rank audacity with wind or gut or ivory? – Outlaws one and all!

After gigs, you push your instruments into instrument-shaped coffins; their peevish whines stifled by velvet and latches shut with a click. Those patient scale-weavers then await your call at which, from the clattering pub din, you will again magic precious, ineffable Music.

17.
The Secret of the Red Lipstick

Melanie Barrow

Why did they have to be enjoying themselves so much? How could they? I watched the ladies chatting animatedly, loading their plates with sandwiches and cakes. I hardly knew them, these friends of Nan's from Whist and Keep Fit.

Unable to bear it any longer, I left the village hall, needing a few minutes on my own. Fat raindrops splashed onto my black dress. 'Sorry, Nan, about the dress.' I whispered. 'You didn't agree with black at funerals, said a funeral should be a celebration of someone's life. But it felt right to me.' I fingered my bright red cardigan. 'This is for you.'

I couldn't believe she'd gone. "Heart attack," the doctor said. "She wouldn't have known a thing. Good way to go."

Why hadn't I visited more often? Nan had always been there for me, and then, when she needed me, I'd been too busy. Tears ran down my cheeks. It had only ever been Nan and me, ever since my parents died in a car crash. Nan who met me at the school gates; put plasters on my grazed knees and cuts. Nan who came to every school fundraiser, every end-of-term concert.

"Sophie?"

An elderly man stood awkwardly looking at me, leaning on his stick.

"These are for you," he held out a soggy bunch of poppies.

"Oh, er ...?"

"Edward. Edward Marsden."

"Thank you, Mr Marsden. That's very kind. Um … how did you know poppies were Nan's favourites?"

"That, my dear, is a long story. One your Nan intended to tell you when you visited."

The last time I visited had been over two months ago. I worked long hours, often at the weekend. It was then she told me there was someone she wanted me to meet; that she'd arrange it for the next time I came home.

There wasn't a next time.

"I hope you don't mind me coming, Sophie. Your nan wanted to introduce me, but …"

"It was so sudden. I didn't even know she was ill."

"She had a weak heart but didn't want to worry you. In any case, she thought she had years left."

"Sorry about your nan, Sophie," a lady with the remains of an ancient perm snaking through hennaed hair interrupted. "She was the life and soul of our group. We'll all miss her."

"Thanks, er …?"

"Mrs Buckell – Elsie. Peggy was wonderful. She could touch her toes and stand on one leg for over five minutes. She even nearly did the splits once, but got stuck halfway! We had to help her up."

I laughed. "She was always better at gymnastics than me. Nice to meet you, Elsie. Please help yourself to food."

When Elsie had left to load her plate – again – I tried to find out more about the stranger. "Nan told me she wanted me to meet someone. Was that you?"

"Can I explain later when this is over? I'm staying at The George for a few days. Is it possible for you to meet me there tomorrow? She gave me something to hand to you in person."

I arrived early, eager to find out more. Walking through the glass revolving doors into the hotel lobby, I saw Edward already ensconced in an overstuffed armchair. A carved wooden box tied up with an ivory satin hair ribbon lay on the table beside him.

"I recognise that ribbon! Nan bought it for my confirmation."

"You were confirmed? I'm surprised."

"Why?"

"Your nan didn't believe in a God who could allow such atrocities to happen."

"How did you….?"

"Let's have something to drink and I'll try to explain. Tea, coffee?"

"Tea, please. Nan said tea helped any problem."

"Pot of tea for two and two toasted teacakes, please," he said to the hovering waiter.

"Why don't you see what's inside the box, Sophie, and then we can talk."

The smell of lavender hit me immediately, a sharp reminder of nan's bedroom. 'Oh, this is the lipstick I found years ago on Nan's dressing table! Isn't it pretty? Why on earth has she kept it all this time?'

"She looked so glamorous wearing it," Edward said dreamily. "Like Vivien Leigh in *Gone With The Wind*."

Smiling at the idea of Nan as Scarlett O'Hara, I pulled

open the bullet-shaped gold art deco tube smothered in tiny stars. Yardley's iconic cherry red.

"This may have been Nan's only red lipstick. I only ever remember her wearing pink or peach. She said red belonged to a different time, but when I was older, she'd tell me the story. Of course, I forgot all about it, selfishly wrapped up in my own life. I never asked again."

Wiping away a tear, I sipped the tea, letting the warm liquid soothe my throat.

Edward gave me a gentle smile. "I'll tell you about the lipstick once you've looked at everything else."

I peered into the box. In the corner lay a ring which seemed to have been made from straw.

"Oh, I remember making that," Edward murmured. "I wanted to give her a token of our time together. All I could find was a willow branch, which I bent into the shape of a ring, wrapping hay around it."

"Ahh, that's so lovely," I said, examining a sepia photo of a man posing by a plane. On the back, in calligraphic writing, was an inscription: *To my Lise. My never-ending gratitude and love.*

"Edward, is that you?"

"Yes. Standing by the Lancaster which got me out of France and back to Blighty. I sent it to your nan, so when she made it home, she'd know I was O.K."

"Why did you call her Lise? Her name was Peggy."

"Lise was her code name.'

"Code name? Wow, what did she do? That sounds so exciting." I suddenly had a thought. "Oh, I wonder if that's why she called Mum, Lisa?"

"I wish I'd met your mum.' He touched my hand. 'I'm

so very sorry about your parents.'

My eyes welled. 'I hardly knew them. I was only five when they were killed. Nan brought me up single-handedly.'

"Peggy was an amazing lady. Look here's her Carte d'Identité. Oh, and open this matchbox. Inside is a tiny hidden camera. Just like James Bond, isn't it?'

"Nan was in the SOE? I've heard about them, but I didn't realise there were women.'

"Yes, she joined the Specials Operations Executive as a secret agent. She went through a rigorous training programme, before being parachuted into France to help the Resistance. Peggy worked mainly as a radio operator, using a radio hidden in a biscuit tin.'

'So that's why Nan's French was so good. Do you know, she made us speak it every mealtime whilst I was doing French O level, and again at A level, even though it meant there were more silences than conversation. There were sticky notes all over the house, labelling things with their French equivalent. I couldn't even open the fridge without seeing one stuck to the milk or the cheese. *Le lait, le fromage.'* I laughed, remembering. 'It's why I chose to read languages at Uni.'

"She told me. She was so proud of you, Sophie. Especially when you got your job as a translator at GCHQ."

"Do you remember her friend, Elsie, saying how agile Nan was? I suppose that was from her training?"

"Yes, although those years in France took their toll. It was May 1942 – I can't believe that's nearly fifty years ago – I'd been on a night-time bombing offensive, trying to take out some factories, and was making for home when a lone Luftwaffe spotted me. I thought I was a gonna. I ducked, but he caught my tail. I tried to steer it towards the ocean, but time was running out. I brought it down in a large cornfield and jumped out just as it burst into flames, rolling as far away as possible. I was in agony. I couldn't move. I knew it was only a matter of time before they found me."

Edward paused to pour another cup of tea.

"When did you meet Nan?" I prompted him.

"Peggy came running out of the surrounding forest, with a small band of men, all wearing dark clothing and navy berets. I didn't realise she was a woman at first. They lifted me onto a stretcher. Everything went black, I must have passed out. The next thing I knew, Peggy was holding a glass of water to my mouth. I tried to get up, but the pain was too much."

"Oh …" I stopped, teacake mid-air, as rich yellow butter oozed onto the plate. 'Sorry, Edward. This is delicious. What happened next?"

"I was petrified the Nazis would find the plane, but Peggy told me the men removed what was left of it. "Best you don't know where," she said. But what she didn't say was, the Nazis, unable to find the plane, torched the neighbouring farm, shooting the farmer's wife and two children in revenge."

I shuddered; it was too horrible to contemplate.

"Days passed in a blur until one day I woke. The sun was shining through the cracked windowpanes, casting a soft glow over the rustic furniture. Vibrant red poppies danced in the breeze. It was as if the world had turned technicolour. Peggy was cooking some sort of stew. The smell of onions made my stomach rumble. She was wearing a red and blue floral dress and a checked headscarf wrapped around her shining brown curls. She must have felt me watching her because she turned and smiled. Such a gorgeous smile. Such beautiful red lips. I fell instantly in love."

"Was it this Yardley lipstick she was wearing?'

"Yes, the very same. If they'd found her, it would have given her away. She said the end of the tube contained a suicide pill – just in case."

I hastily put it down.

Edward chuckled. "Don't worry, it was emptied ages ago. Where was I? Oh, yes. That was the day I felt better. It was also the day I realised I loved her. I didn't want to endanger her any longer and asked her to make arrangements to get me out of France. Then we heard the sound we'd dreaded – the stutter of a car engine, as it snaked its way down the dirt track to the farmhouse. Quickly she hid the radio, and then removing an old rug, pulled up some floorboards. Below was a makeshift room. She helped me down a ladder and covered me in old sacks. I was in total darkness, forced to keep quiet. I've never been so terrified in all my life."

Edward put his head in his hands, waiting for his breathing to calm down.

"Peggy was amazing. So calm. She told the German soldier, in what sounded like impeccable French, that she'd come to visit her mother's cousin, only the farm was empty when she arrived. She'd been to the village for some provisions and was staying a couple of days before going home. I'm not sure how much the German understood, but I heard him reply: *Du bist sehr schön Fräulein* – you're very beautiful – and what sounded like a scuffle. Edward paused, taking out an ironed white handkerchief to wipe his forehead. "It was the hardest thing I've ever done, staying still and not pushing my way up to help her, but it would have meant her death sentence."

"Oh …" I mouthed, hardly able to believe he was talking about Nan.

"Fortunately, it wasn't long before Peggy came down to check on me. She told me the remains of the plane had been discovered and the German was summoned to round up the poor villagers." He cleared his throat. "We'd been lucky at the expense of others."

Edward looked at me, a slight colour rising in his cheeks. "Peggy was shaking. I put my arms around her, and we sat like that for a while, until suddenly we were kissing. And er … well … you probably don't need to hear what happened next."

I considered what he said. "Nan told me Grandad was shot down in the war and died. Did she meet him after you left …? Or …? Oh, wow, are you …?"

"Yes Sophie, I'm your grandad. But I never knew until recently."

I felt stunned. All these secrets. Why hadn't Nan told me?

"A few nights later, one of the men from the Maquis – the Resistance – came to give me instructions. I was being lifted back to England." Edward reached out to grasp my hands. "You must believe me; I had no idea Peggy was pregnant."

"But why didn't you try to find her after the war?"

"This is the part I'm ashamed of. I was married – and yes, your nan knew – but you have to understand we were living through impossible times. Each day could be our last. The love we found in that broken-down farmhouse was magical. A slice of heaven in a hellish world. But I had a wife at home and responsibilities. I sent that photo and tried to forget. Two years later, my wife and I had a daughter and life went on."

"How did you meet Nan again?"

"My wife died five years ago and after a few months passed, I started wondering about Peggy. I didn't want to complicate her life, so put off trying to find her. One day, I told my daughter Anne – named after Annecy, near where I was shot down. She encouraged me to write to Peggy. So, I did – this letter here." He pulled from his pocket an envelope marked, "address unknown."

"We moved," I explained. 'Not far. To a barn conversion. Nan didn't want to stay in town once my parents died. She craved open space."

"A barn conversion?" Edward said, a smile hovering around his lips. "How appropriate! I'd love to see it. She invited me for tea but …"

"Of course. I want to show you everything – her house, the village, her life here. I can't believe I have a grandad." I leaned across and gave him a quick kiss on his weathered cheek. "How did you trace her, eventually?"

"I went to your old street on the off chance someone remembered her. I nearly gave up, when a lady at no.4 said, yes, she knew Nancy very well. Apparently, they met up at a whist drive once a month. So, mustering as much courage as possible, I phoned her."

"Wow!"

"I know. I felt like a teenager on a first date. We met

here at The George for tea and toasted teacakes. I sat here, in this same armchair. I was far too early. But then Peggy stepped through the doors. It was as if the last fifty years hadn't happened. There was my darling Peggy, as beautiful as ever. She wore a knee-length red dress with little white flowers and a white cardigan. And, yes, she was wearing red lipstick." He shook his head as I looked at him questioningly. "No, I don't think it could have been the same one, unfortunately, it would have dried up by now. We talked for so long, we stayed for lunch and into the early evening." His voice cracked as he reached for a handkerchief.

I touched his arm. 'She shouldn't have passed so soon. It's not fair, not just as you met again."

"I had one more lunch with her when she gave me this box. She wanted to introduce me properly, but now I think she must have had a premonition."

"Do you have grandchildren?" I tried to lighten the mood.

He relaxed. 'Yes, two. Both boys."

"Can I meet them sometime? I thought I had no one and now I have a granddad and some sort of step-family. It's amazing!"

One month later, I was in France, gazing at a cornfield covered in poppies. Edward and his daughter, Anne, on either side of me. The farmhouse had been replaced by a smart hotel complex complete with a swimming pool.

"It's hard to believe it's the same place." Edward said. "Except for the forest and the poppy field, I wouldn't have recognised it."

I stared at the scarlet heads bobbing in the warm breeze.

"Bye, Nan. I miss you." The ashes caught in the wind, settling amongst the poppies.

"Bye Lise – Peggy. I wish we'd had more time together." Edward blew his nose.

"You should write their story one day,' Anne said, putting her arm through mine. "A story of bravery and lost love."

I smiled. "A story of a red lipstick and its secret."

18.
Are You Alright?

James Armstrong

In some time
           we haven't talked, head to heart. Are you
sleeping through the night these days; coping the everyday
toughs – gas bill; fettle; ought tos; joys? When in a fix of
yours,
or another's, making, do you appeal to an acquaintance,
barman, solicitor? Is there any one thing
                                 I might do?
Then:
        I casually turned to say…   you'd taken off
with a few commonplaces: I'll be fine; overandout –
your fledgling trip still more flappy, crash-bounces than
airborne – left on the first fair wind waving;
assumed you weren't
                drowning.
Once:
        I was your whole picture: five-bar gate, picnickers
harbour in the bay, weathers. Wasn't as though not
foretold: I count now, as a once-in-a-while thin light
losing a scrap with time; a wisp of slipstream
peeling from a vehicle
                going west.
Then:
        too, I was always tearing off, somewhere –
no glance aft to check you were in tow; my own plans
in view. Too often abandoned you: supposed

you OK – 'inadvertently' is no excuse – so:
you found your own foreground,

                      weather, picnic.
Now:
     do you have that someone to hold your thimble;
wield your needle; sew your wounds, patch your
failures; smooth down triumphs; kept by you
those warm-inside somethings for when you can't even
fathom the 3-card trick:
                 chocolate; planting things;
                 your forearm touched.
Here:
     life without you is just plain weird.
Life without you is far worse
               than feared

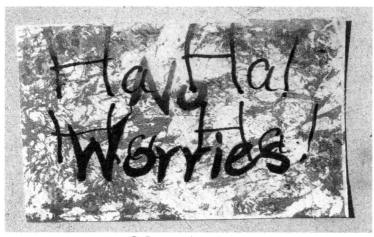

© James Amstrong

19.
When The Lights Went Out

Graham Bishop

The four of them had spent a pleasant three days in the bustling port of Paimpol on the north Brittany coast. It was a typical Breton harbour with a mix of fishing boats, a modern yacht marina and a fleet of tourist trip boats. One of the spectacular local sights which they could just see from the marina was a small island or very large rock depending on your point of view over which circled a huge flock of gannets. The flashes of the birds dive-bombing fish in the deep waters round the rock was one of nature's wonders. No wonder the French call them Fous, mad.

Their trip along the Breton coast had been an adventure, a test of navigation. The coastline was strewn with rocks, many just below the surface, seemingly swirled in all directions by currents and counter currents. The weather had been kind and the welcomes ashore even kinder. They had discovered Calvados, strong and fruity; Pommeau, a smooth aperitif channelling its name with Pineau from much further south; and more recently Lambig de Bretagne from the nearby town of Lannion, another 40% proof version of cider.

They had all succumbed to the blue and white stripes of the sweaters and T shirts of the area and the two men clichédly wore Breton sailors' caps. They felt they were living in a different dimension, warm, hazy, nourished on fruits de mer, crêpes and galettes. Their skin bristled with salt, their hair was bleached a lighter shade than normal, their faces sun and wind weathered. A perfect getaway break.

When they left the harbour that evening for the night sail back to their home port of Noss Mayo in Devon, conversation flowed freely. The stars were just beginning to appear and the moonrise was only a couple of hours away. Behind them the lights on the shore picked out the houses in the harbour. Then more pinpoints of light appeared on the cliff tops on either side. The further out they sailed the fewer the lights twinkled, both below on the waterline and above on the cliffs. Finally the luminous thread attaching them to the shore was extinguished.

The skipper went forward to check the port, starboard and masthead lights. All in order. Back in the cockpit the cabin doors were open and the yellow light from below illuminated the helm and the compass on its gimbled mounting forward of the wheel. The smell of mackerel frying reached him, but he called out to them to pull the doors to. He needed to restore his night vision now that they were moving out towards the shipping lanes. But he didn't refuse the mackerel buttie when it was passed up to him. Nor the coffee later.

Scudding clouds silhouetted black against the light of the moon crossed in front of it and he could feel the wind rising. A deeper darkness enveloped the ketch. The crossing would last at least 18 hours. Fortunately the main hazards – cargo ships and ferries – were lit up like buses. The skipper had crossed the Channel several times. He knew the dangers, he knew the way. He was sorry the moon had hidden itself. At least the lights of the passing ships stood

out more sharply as they headed down the Channel towards
the Atlantic, or up the Channel to the ports of the North
Sea and the Baltic. He just needed to gauge their speed and
to set the course to avoid them.

Every two hours one of the others emerged from the
cabin and took over the helm after a short briefing on their
position; on the compass heading. Moonset would not be
for another six hours, but there was no moonlight now
anyway and the stars had retired behind the clouds. The
course across was not straight. The tides in the Channel
were strong and crossing them diagonally meant being
swept down towards the Isles of Scilly for six hours and
then being swept back up east for six hours cancelling out
the drift.

High up on the bridge checking the radar screen, the
Captain of the container ship heading up Channel at a
steady 25 knots demanded urgently to know why the
dimmed coms lights had gone out. And why the outside
navigation lights had failed. He realised they were making
passage blacked out and blind in one of the busiest
waterways in the world. Against all the rules. Against all
common sense. Get the emergency lighting on. And fast, he
ordered.

Way below his sight-line the ketch and his ship were
closing fast. The Captain sensed rather than felt a slight
bump. A judder. He opened the door of the bridge and
peered out across the darkness. There was nothing to be
seen.

20.
Pain

Helen Connor

A difficult pain
original or referred?
No bruises to show
no cuts and no bleeding
Shifting, stretching,
try to ease the cause
Hidden, sneaking
Invisible pain
The aching pain of tears and anger
Feelings buried, deep as the coal.
Emotions erupting,
crumpled as tissues
Twisted, disabling
Frustrating pain.
This remembered pain
Fractured relationships across cavernous
distances
Words said and unsaid
filling the cracks
Nodding politeness
Recurring pain.
This transferred pain
Impacting on others
Losses that burn
fall as ash in the wind

Anthology

Raising of voices,
silently weeping
A pain that is fragile,
close to the edge
Pain that is whispered,
Pain that is screamed,
Pain that can torture,
Pain that leaves scars,
Pain needing surgery,
Pain wanting a kiss
to make it all better.
Sticking plasters to cover....
Which pain is yours?

21.
The Crash Scene

Alyson Hilbourne, Prize Winner

See …

… the straight road, lined with sentinel spruces, the lorry, jack-knifed across it like a

wounded animal, the driver's white face looming behind the windscreen.

… the car overturned on the verge, bonnet crumpled, one wheel spinning forlornly

in the air.

… a child's plush toy dinosaur, its paint box colours gaudy on the grey tarmac.

… the police car arrive, the young constable view the scene and suck in his breath.

Taste …

… the ferrous tang as the constable bites his lip. His first accident scene. His first

day out alone.

… bile rising sourly in his throat. He swallows and girds himself to investigate.

What will he find? Could anyone survive?

He turns off the siren and steps out of his car.

Smell …

… the resinous aroma from the trees, reminding him of family Christmases, a warm

room, fairy lights and presents stacked under the tree.

… a sharp chemical odour that tickles inside his nose and sticks to the back of his throat.

Something is leaking.

He gives an involuntary shudder and bounds towards the car.

Hear…

… boots crunch on the tarmac.

"Wasn't my fault, mate. She came out of nowhere." The lorry driver stands beside

him.

The constable looks up. The driver's eyes are dilated, his skin pale. His forehead

carries a slick sheen.

Shock, the constable thinks, but his attention is on the overturned vehicle.

"Can you help?" he asks.

The shadow of the car driver, trapped upside down by the seat belt is visible through the splintered windscreen.

He grips the door handle and pulls.

"Come on!"

He tugs and braces a foot against the side panel.

The sharp click as the door releases echoes round the trees. He takes the woman's weight as the lorry driver releases the clasp. Together they half lift, half drag her from the car. A jammy smudge of blood congeals on her forehead.

Laid on the grass, she opens her eyes, and starts, searching for something she cannot see.

"My baby!" Her shrill voice slices through the forest silence.

He breathes deeply to slow the hammering in his chest.

A baby?

He didn't see a child.

He approaches the car again, the smell of fuel stronger.

The forest is brooding, the quiet oppressive. He swallows and licks his lips.

Anthology

The rear passenger door is open.

A wail, like an alarm, engages from somewhere beyond the vehicle, low at first and

cranking up to a higher, fiercer pitch.

Before he can move, the air around him is sucked away, in a loud whoosh, as the car erupts in flames.

Heat tries to scald him as he circles it, eyes stinging, to find still strapped in a car seat, a toddler, face twisted in fury, fists tight, mouth opening for another yell.

Angry, but alive.

Feel …

… relief hit him like an uppercut, making him stagger.

For a moment he shuts his eyes, letting the warmth of the flames wash over him, before he releases the catch and lifts the writhing toddler into his arms …

22.
Damsel

James Armstrong

We stuttered down a sharp, switchback incline and spilled onto the beach; approached the group: new acquaintances with two daughters in loungers; dark and fair. The dark girl: striking features; studying her nails, confident. The blonde: slight, wary; eyes and thoughts breezing about.

The kind of day: no sooner sunbathe-hot than clouds palm the sun proving the chill-wind's effect. Sunbathing: studying the always engrossing sea; its shifty, quilted surface, emblazoned with startling colours: secret blues, milky-greens, acid-yellows – all lain beneath a cliff-face of inflamed foliage. I relish the sounds of bickering sea-birds, adults playing children's games; children learning childhood skills like being caught out, not knowing the rules and losing.

'How old are you both?' The dark one, 'I'm sixteen. She's twenty one, can you believe?' The blonde: no defensive retort, just blithely smiles. I ask about school, jobs, uni. The dark girl says, 'Criminology.' 'Mmm. An unusual choice.' 'I think it'll be interesting.' 'So you want to be a criminal?' A small smile. Not funny, even to a sixteen year old.

I swim and return. 'Why not go in? It's really not cold.' The fair one, submerged under a rug: 'I like to be warm.' She presents as an untutored 12 year-old, a betwixt and between. Unprompted, she approaches the water, new-born foal like. A breeze, metaphorical or not, could waft her up and drop her down, dislocated in mind or limb, in a place, fathomless. Her glance zips about like a damsel fly: no manifest pattern. I feed her stones to skim; smiles leak from her eyes and cheeks. 'Five times. Hee, hee, hee,' she peeps, thrilled at skipping a stone. She's a natural: no crook-armed 'girl's throw'. Scampers back to her rug.

A bolt of knowing grips me: here is sheer innocence, unmarked. Here is an angelette, who can't hold onto more than one feeling at once, struggling to make sense of this place called 'living'.

Later, up top, our group are clustered near a kiosk. She's standing nearby; idle: 'Don't want an ice-cream.' Her moves skittering in tune with her own thought-trains? At odd times, she attends to outer sights: unabashed, she latches her whole gaze on tracking two passers-by. Curious? surprised? In wonderment that something could happen; that anything does happen, and this minute, in the sun, on any street, on a cliff-top. From nothing, she moves to her mum; sneaks her hand through her parent's palm, lolls her head on her mother, fawning, as a three year old, or a Siamese kitten might – just a few, brief, needed seconds then gone: slips five metres away from us all – looking down, studying. Is she watching her own, potent Harvest Moon rising or a densely sprinkled Milky Way, where we see but dull tarmac? She carries her own illumination – her glow outshines this luminous, August late-afternoon.

This minute, basking in her radiance, it's difficult to picture a black side. There must be many moments to threaten her existence? Hyper-sensitive, she recoils from every hostile message her inbuilt radar detects; she must respond to the numbing klaxon-howl with her inner nugget of self-preservation. Then, her behaviours would be ultimate, last-ditch, to avoid her extinction. At these times, any and every action will be valid in her sanctum law: tantrums, biting, screaming, smashing things… Who knows how black her black can become?

She's had an obstacled, beaten track through school – through jobs. Never mind! She already came with a job. It's called 'being' – surviving every keen, smarting minute and the next – and they keep coming and she must keep examining them. But sometimes, there are too many of them for one small girl and they happen too fast and she must still keep batting them off. She will shriek, abscond; deny all contact – block all entrances, scan for exits – hide under a rug; regroup. All activity must cease until she reclaims her comfort.

We toughened-by-life souls may be surviving; have we lost something in the process, though? – that hard-fought for, alive-every-second sensation – have we sacrificed our first acceptance to the invasion of new sensations which yet can be barbarous painful? Some things felt are so bang-fresh, they confirm life with a tingle, renew life even, with a quiver but at what cost to the wear on our senses? Many of us inlay a veneer like Formica to inure ourselves from such excoriating exposure.

Anthology

Some few are unable, others unwilling, to forego that relentless assault on the red-raw senses. They accept the coarse pain which experience demands as equally they enjoy the ecstasy of inhaling clean morning air or tasting the first, sweet and tart flavour of zest from a pomegranate.

Artists valiantly give witness to life as ever-new in their works; scientists examine material things afresh. Designers look askance at previous solutions. But are they second best to the guiltless angels who land once in a random while, on an everyday street, as living examples, plainly pointing us down the road to our untainted self? These seraphs don't need to compose music or poems; design cities, discover cures. They live and endure every fresh minute entire. Are they prototypes of being in the world: the first Adams or Eves? Maybe this is how purity, showering over us, feels? Be blessed in their presence if your life is lucky enough to be illuminated by just one of these tender Tinkerbelles.

Saint George, Damsel and Dragon (c. 1470),
Paolo Uccello.
Tempera on wood, 52 x 90 cm
Musée Jacquemart-André, Paris.

23.
Wenna's Walls

Max Bowler, Prize Winner

No one remembered why the walls were built, no one wished to leave either. No one except Wenna.

Wenna was still young, but her bright black eyes looked weary. She wore a rough cloak that floated over her thin, bony body and her long hair hung lifelessly, soaking wet from her walk in the rain on their hunt for food.

'You must follow the rules, the rules keep you alive,' commanded Wenna's mother.

Wenna knew the rules off by heart.

1. No one can leave the forest.

2. Never go outside of the cave after the sun goes down.

3. No asking questions.

But Wenna had asked many questions, until her mother had become angry and stopped speaking at all. Her mother meant well but her words were sometimes unkind. Wenna wondered about the mysterious scars on her mother's back or why her mother never allowed her to go out alone, and the strange noises that she heard outside in the darkness of the night.

Until that night, the night when Wenna woke up with a jolt. Her ears pricked up at the strange shrieking sounds coming from outside her cave. Cautiously, Wenna crawled out of her rough straw bed and tiptoed towards the entrance to the cave. She held her breath, looked back at her mother sleeping in her bed and swiftly left her home.

24.
The Lost Parable

An imaginative story

Grenville Gilbert

Archaeologists, excavating in an area close to the Temple wall in East Jerusalem, think that they have discovered the Narrow Gate (1), referred to in the Gospel according to St Matthew. Carbonised splinters of wood, found in two post holes, suggest the previous existence of some form of gate or door. The width of the opening is such that it would have been possible for a person, or, unladen beast of burden, to just about squeeze through it. At the same time, it would have been possible to close the opening quickly, if events necessitated. Carbon dating indicates that the gate or door was in existence at around 50 BC. What are more interesting are the artefacts found on the site; a brooch in the shape of a fish, an oil lamp, a cup and, of particular interest, a small wine flagon, containing a complete papyrus sheet. Clearly, the papyrus sheet had been part of an early Christian book. The language is Aramaic. The sheet of papyrus is headed 'Parable of the non-believer'. A modern translation might be 'Parable of the atheist'. In the narrative, Jesus was walking in the area of Jerusalem known as Gethsemane, near the Mount of Olives (2), shortly before his trial and crucifixion, when he stopped to tell the following parable:-

"There was a man, whom it was rumoured, did not believe in the existence of God. One day, the man was walking in this very area, when a Pharisee, who worshipped regularly in the Temple, asked him straight out 'Do you believe in the existence of God?' The man looked the Pharisee directly in the eye and answered with another question. 'See that old olive tree over there; how do you know that it exists?' The Pharisee responded immediately, 'Because I can see and touch it.' 'There you have my answer' said the man. The man and the Pharisee parted company. The Pharisee went off into the Temple to offer a small sacrifice, thanking God that he was not like the man who did not believe in the existence of God. Meanwhile, the man proceeded on up the mountainside and into the secluded garden, where he opened his heart and soul to the God he perceived to be within him and within all creation. He meditated. 'How can God be outside of creation, as some kind of supernatural, all-powerful being, viewing everything he has created as good (3), and, at the same time, be accessible to us human beings within that creation. We can, literally, know absolutely nothing of such a God, as such a God would be external to creation! If God is to be known, then surely God has to be of the same existence of which we are a part, and not outside of creation? It would be like talking about the existence of another form of existence, about which we can know and experience nothing! The simplest and most satisfactory way of thinking about God, is as Existence itself. To then speak of God as existing would make no sense. Existence cannot, surely, exist? Therefore, logically, God cannot exist. It would be like saying that God is love and expecting love to love; again, it makes no sense. In the man's mind, the conventional disconnect between God and creation also meant that all Temple worship was idolatrous; worshippers were only thinking of themselves and what things a completely imaginary, external God, whom they slavishly worshipped, could do for them. They would be failing to love the God of Existence, through loving one another and through loving the whole of creation. Surely, thought the man, we all live and move and have our being in God (4). After meditating, the man looked around and saw God in everything and everyone, including the self-righteous Pharisee! That made a lot more sense to him; being able to love God in such a way. He felt at one with God; what he called at-one-ment. He could see that, in the end, it mattered not that you believed that God might or might not exist. The Pharisee's question was meaningless and purposeless. The important thing was to love, because God is love (5); that, he thought, is true worship. The test for us is to see if love works: action was far more important and relevant than mere belief.

After having told his disciples the parable, Jesus walked on into the very same garden to which he had just been referring. Like the man in the parable, he felt God and himself to be one, sufficient, even, to refer to God as 'Father' (6). Jesus felt deeply for all those trapped in the idolic and lifeless ways of the Temple. Peter and the two sons of Zebedee went with him into the garden but, a little further on, Jesus instructed them to remain where they were and to keep watch (7). Jesus then walked a little way ahead and fell on his face and prayed (8). In his heart and in his head, he knew where it was all going to lead. He was only too aware that with love comes pain and suffering and, even, death."

Quite a discovery, a parable hidden for all those years in a wine flagon! Ironically, its discovery has the potential for being a real game-changer, at a time when the Church needs something radical and credible in order to halt its decline. You might think it paradoxical that the discovery was made outside of the city walls and away from the Temple; what you might describe as the Church of its day. It makes you start to think more about the role of the Narrow Gate in St Matthew's account; was it a metaphor for enclosure or escape, for security or for freedom? Was Jesus comparing the Narrow Gate with all the other gates into the city which were a great deal wider, making the road to the Temple that much easier, albeit, meaningless, to take? Then there is the passage in St Matthew's account immediately before the Narrow Gate section (9). It describes the Golden Rule which is found in all of the world's main religions; do to others as you would have them do to you! Jesus saw this as a precis of all of the law and the prophets. Even more radical perhaps, the question has to be asked, does the lost parable contain the very essence of the Gospel message that has been misrepresented by the Church for the last 2000 years? Did Jesus intend that God should be understood as love, such that we are all able to know God for ourselves through our own individual acts of love? Is the Kingdom of Heaven a present-day Kingdom of love (10)? Is God about active living and not about passive worship? Put another way: is it in 'living through loving' that we can practice the true wor(th)ship of God? No wonder we can't see and touch God; God, all along, has been with us(11)! God is a quality of being; not a being! More a verb than a noun! Through love, we find ourselves at one with the very consciousness of God! The parable also raises deeper questions; did Jesus foresee how the Church would massage his Gospel message, so as to turn it into a sin/guilt/power machine, based, falsely, on revelation, authority and patriarchy. In essence, did Jesus teach a judgemental belief system, or, a way to life, based on compassion, forgiveness and unconditional love? I can only leave you to make up your own minds. Amazing what you discover in an old wine flagon!

For those who like to explore biblical references:-

(1) Matthew 7 vv 13&14; (2) Matthew 26 v 36; (3) Genesis 1; (4) Acts 17 vv 27&28 (5) 1 John 4 vv 7&8; (6) Luke 23 v 34 and, John 1 v 18; (7)Matthew 26 vv 37-39; (8) Matthew 26 v 39; (9) Matthew 7 v 12; (10) Luke 17 vv 20 & 21; and, (11) Matthew 1 v 23. The Lost Parable

25.
Breakfast

Graham Bishop

She poured the water into the coffee pot
He put the coffee pot on the table
She poured the coffee into the cups
He got up to fetch the milk
He doesn't take milk
Maybe a splash of goat's milk
He ate his muesli
She doesn't eat muesli
She put the slice into the toaster
He put the toast on the table
She placed her hand on the table
He covered her hand with his hand
Hand on hand on the table
She looked into his eyes
He looked into her eyes
She smiled at him
He smiled at her
He said it without saying it.
She said without saying it: I know

With acknowledgments to Prévert

26.
Inkling

James Armstrong

A long day's fiddle instruction in the shire. The composer
cycled home.
'I'm drained, Alice.'
'Dear, dear – and drenched.' She smiled, teasing off his wet
coat.
'Not a minim left in me.'

After dinner, he lights up a cigar, perches on a stool.
Lays an arm across the ebonised Steinway, his mood palls;
he stares inwardly at the keyboard; unwinds. His wife clears
the lamp-lit table; the wick whispers; her cream bustle
creaks.

He meanders down lanes among the staves and Malvern
scenes;
hills shift closer, clouds of smoke perfume the room,
sift over the figure poring over his instrument. In time,

little trinkets of sounds mooch around, falling onto sofas
and surfaces; cling to curtains; disappear into the matt
October shadows. Fanciful reveries prevail – under my feet,
coarse quitches primeval hills, swift-vaulting clouds, pink
whinberry scent, indistinct bird chants; wanton windsong

feathers my cheeks – Alice brushes off crumbs and the
landed scraps of notes from the tablecloth.

He draws on his Havana, taps ash from its tip;
breathes half-measures, pauses;
exhales two semi-breves – 'ah, ah; – aaah, aaah.'

Nursing the keys – no more –
veils of blue-grey reign,
Alice smoothing out the crinkled damask,
startles at a particular sequence of flutes
and intervals. Stops.
'I like that tune, Edward; play it again.'

Looking up through the haze, woken
from wherever he was – 'Eh! What tune?'
returns to coaxing a pulse from the impassive ivories

listening for anything familiar:
Alice, glistening crumb-pan in hand, waiting;
cigar: ignored, in its crystal tray, burning…

Trickles of notes begin to string together
like a skein of late geese flying westwards
through the layered cloud-drifts in the room.

'That's it. That's the tune.'

Anthology

© James Armstrong

27.
Core Blimey
Richard Lappas

Is that the apple of my eye, all shiny and crisp looks worth a
try
They say very healthy and easy to see why.
An apple a day is what the Doctors say
Healthier than that choc bar saying work, rest and play

First bite as it feels flavour with a deafening crunch
No doubting its a hell of a munch
Its been said that the core is meant to be best
so suggest you pick up and give it a test

Eat the core its not mushy or slimy
you will love the taste and think core blimey

28.
Unravelled Life

Rosemary Gemmell, Prize Winner

Ellen picked up the tiny pearl, translucent with promise, a perfect sphere. Fashioning an eight knot to secure the bead, she threaded the next pearl, taking her time to admire her work. She looped the thread once then brought the end over and under, tightening it to form the knot to hold this one in place.

Her mistress expected perfection even now.

Pausing to dash a sudden tear from tired eyes as her work was nearing its end, Ellen tried not to think of the coming days. She had been a good and loyal seamstress to her young mistress, mending rich fabrics that had protected the wearer from cold castles and hard rides over rough ground. Sewing elaborate Turk's head knots to attach small buttons on silken gowns for grander affairs.

How could a life unravel so completely? Like the unpicked hems of the little girl who had returned from foreign shores, promised a kingdom that now proved her undoing.

Ellen stood to rub her lower back before her mistress returned from the short daily walk that was her only release from the imprisonment she now faced. Ellen knew of the ill-fated marriages, of the courtly plots and political turbulence. But most of all she appreciated the tall, noble woman who loved her people, who showed kindness to those undeserving of it, and who allowed tolerance in worship that many denied.

Lifting the pearl-studded headdress, Ellen set it aside for approval, admiring the way the scant light from the narrow window illuminated each bead. She picked up the favourite pearls that would never again encircle the pale slender neck at courtly balls and colourful pageants. It lay heavy and cold in her gnarled, knotted fingers, swollen with age and intricate sewing tasks.

Hearing light footsteps approaching the door, Ellen waited.

Her mistress seemed in good spirits today, pacing about the room as though her energy could not be contained in such a small space.

"It is such a beautiful day, Ellen, that I wanted to ride across the countryside, the wind tugging at my hair, the sun on my face, thawing this ice gripping my heart. Why do they still lock me up when I mean my cousin no harm?"

Ellen stood silently, while her mistress removed her warm plaid and settled in her chair once more. No answer was expected, but she always listened with discretion and love for the girl who waited in vain for freedom.

"Pass me my embroidery, please, Ellen. I see you have finished securing the pearls to my headdress. Thank you."

Ellen curtsied and passed the embroidery and threads, for her mistress was as fine a needlewoman as any.

"I must finish this before..."

Mary's voice faltered for the first time, as Ellen watched her sew the next French knot that showed her fine stitching. And her heart broke for this beautiful young woman, Queen of Scots, whose life would end too soon in cruel execution.

29.
It May be Futile

Annabelle Harper, Prize Winner

Emma's pen pattered against the desk in a sporadic rhythm as she rested her chin in her other hand, slouching in defeat while her eyes drifted to the window. Through the glass, a lone sparrow fluttered about the chain link fence that separated the school from the outside world. It danced and bounced on intangible platforms, daring to get closer and closer with every flap. Eventually its game of cat and mouse with the stationary object came to an end as the small bird darted through the gap.

Well, it tried to fly. It tried to dash through the diamond shaped hole. It tried to leave. Emma didn't quite understand how it'd happened but her head perked up slightly and posture straightened in anticipation as the little creature managed to wedge itself between the wiring. She could see the sparrow still momentarily in shock. Complete paralysis overtaking it. She watched in fascination as the realisation of its predicament settled in like morning dew. She could almost feel the panic and dread begin to rise, and rise it did.

The little bird beat its wings experimentally, once, twice - brown and black speckled feathers slowly increasing their tempo, testing the limits of its freedom. Then it grew frantic. Its wings mocked a hummingbird as it thrashed its

119

tiny body, delicate feet clawing at the sleek plastic. The tapping of Emma's pen accelerated in tandem with the bird, sympathetic background music to its struggle.

Her face was blank despite the pitiful scene. She really should've been paying attention to her teacher, droning on and on about the importance of quadratics, but the sparrow commanded her attention with the same level of mercy it received from the stoic fence. She couldn't wrench her eyes away from the embodiment of futility, its endless endeavour to be free, and eternal perseverance gaining it nothing but exhaustion and pain. The window was closed, but she could see the wailing chirps that would've spilled from its open beak. It wriggled uselessly, trapped between the bars of a cage not meant for it.

Pitiful yet mesmerising.

Eventually the bird slowed and with it, Emma's morbid interest dwindled. Her hand grew tired and she slowed the sympathetic battering of her pen. Turning the other cheek to the now dull sparrow in favour of algebraic equations. The teacher was now handing out worksheets they had to complete for homework. Emma wondered what the canteen would have for lunch. There was only twenty minutes left of the lesson and the walls of the classroom weren't getting any more interesting with the passage of time.

Only a passing thought held questions of the unfortunate sparrow's survival. Maybe the caretaker would spot it and free it. She didn't bother wasting any glances out the window, where she was sure it hadn't yet given up. Ten minutes later, she finally stopped tapping her pen.

30.
Peacock Kite

Cheryl Burman, Prize Winner

The boy is too small. The kite too big.

Blustering squalls which whip the grasses sloping to the cliff edge tumble the kite through a louring evening sky like a nest-less fledgling. Its ribboned tail tangles in a snarl of colours. The boy clings to the line, arms tight against its drag. His head bobs, keeping time with his flying toy.

I squint into the wind. Where is the father who this morning laughed with this boy on the sunny beach, guiding his small hands on the line?

Petrichor had hung in the air, as much proof of the passed shower as the glistering drops which turned the sea thrift to pink tourmaline. I had stooped to gather the rosette-hearted flowers, curious if their semblance to the jewel might keep the devils in their hells. For a time. Roused by a child's joyous shriek, I lifted my head to find the father, son, and the glorious kite. Peacock-shaped, brilliant wings outstretched, its tail feathers coursed across a fresh-washed sky.

Turning back to my gathering, my hand hovered over the tempting yellow poison of horned poppy. No. I touched a finger to my 'tourmaline' and snipped grey fronds of wormwood. Healing fronds, pressed to cuts and bruises. Should they be called for.

The boy had run along the sand, the kite filling his

world. The father proffered me a quick glance and strode away.

Now, on the cliff top, a tumultuous wind eddies around the kite, tosses it higher, still higher. The kite surges, falls, gorging on the gusts to soar above the white-capped waves thundering against the rocks below. Gulls rise from their nests, screeching reproof.

The boy's eyes are fixed on the kite. His feet slither on wet grass, legs taut, body unbalanced. The peacock wings swallow the turbulence, swelling and collapsing in imitation of the billowing waves. They yank the boy, tugging, hauling him towards the gulls – towards the plummeting drop.

Four more stumbling steps. Three. Two …

"Let go! I scream against the wind. Let go!"

He cannot let go, cannot escape the kite's unrelenting drag. The boy is as ensnared as a fish on a worm-laden hook.

No time to ponder, to consider the consequences of confirmation.

I spread my arms, body lifting … and I am flying … fighting the storm … arms braced, fingers clawed to pluck and save …

31.
Coleridge Bridge

David Kerr

The morning ritual of taking my daughter to the school bus stop had become a nature trail. This morning, sentinel rabbits and friendly robins occupied our attention and distracted us from the downpour, it was hard to curse nature when the azure flash of kingfishers flickered in the peripheral vision. The Otter valley rain gave the impression of a living, breathing creature and fell as if the heavens were being drained of all their water. It bounced on the tarmac of the Coleridge bridge while over East Hill the sun leaked red fire through rifts in the grey clouds so that half the sky blazed as if God had bled across the heavens. The other half, all to the west, was shrouded in grey clouds. It was as though that same god had dragged a blanket half way across the vale as if to confirm my deepest instinct that the universe exists in opposition to itself. I was witnessing nature's yin yang.

We stop to look in to the river, hoping to see the shadow of a trout, or a dace, or the real prize, an otter. The rain obscures the river surface view, breaking up the picture into an absurd gleaming mosaic and shielding the target from our alien eyes. Another flash of blue, I feel honoured to get the glimpse and smile as the rain drops onto my nose from the peak of my flat cap. My daughter laughs as I wipe the water off of my nose and leave a trail of green moss residue on my face, picked up from the bridge's rail. It's fine, the rain will cleanse me, wiping the slate clean.

Dog walkers hurry by, some in glistening colourful cagoules. On another day they would stop for a chat but today I am happy that they do not as I'm deep in communication with God. I wonder if the passing dogs can appreciate the morning's spectacle. Or is it a blessing reserved for God's human children, a reward to dilute the hardships and anxieties. I mention to Maya that there should be a rainbow, but there is not. This morning doesn't need one. I wonder if my emotion is driven by the morn's glory or if I was already primed to see and feel the best of all things regardless of aesthetics. Sometimes my mind can find beauty in anything, sometimes in very little. Maybe my mind is a reflection of the bi-polar sky, grey and light fighting a battle for eternity. For my lifetime at least.

It's time to move on and get my daughter to the bus stop. I wave to her as the bus drives away and think about the walk back across the Coleridge bridge again. I decide to take another route, if perfection exists, I had just experienced it in that moment past and etched it onto my soul.

Maybe I'll write about it one day.

32.
Jennifer Simpson

Bob Sillitoe

Tucked away off a small one-way road in the city, Wonford
Road, and down a small track, Rectory Lane, only a short
walk from the row of shops called 'the village' two
bungalows had been squeezed into what was the garden of
the old rectory building. It's garden large enough for the
Vicar to run his model steam railway around on fete day
each year. Giving youngsters a ride for a few pence to help
boost the dwindling accounts of St Anthony's Church half a
mile away.

Much had changed from those days in the nineteen
seventies when the two bungalows were originally built. The
land sold off to developers under strict instructions from
the church the homes were for the retired and no one else.

Andreas stood at the front door of number 2 Rectory
Bungalow and waited. Straining to see through the obscure
glass of the front door. One which he had installed a year
ago after being contacted by Jennifer Simpson. It was the
second job he had carried out for her. His first was soon
after Jennifer moved in and wanted the kitchen converted.
She wanted all the worktop lowered. Only being short, she
did not want to struggle around the kitchen, always over
stretching, and it was what she was used to. Andreas had
been called in to take out the old and put in a brand new
specially made kitchen for her.

Jenny's enthusiasm and liveliness struck a chord with Andreas. How she managed to stay fit and healthy in her retirement years, always with a positive spin on life. And although losing her husband, Neville, two and a half years ago, her spirits were always high and Andreas had a love and respect for her. Neville was considerably older than Jenny, passing away in his sleep at the age of eighty-five. Somewhat expected but still a shock for Jenny and her family.

Selling up their detached family home, lived in for forty-one years was heart wrenching. The home where she raised her family, two daughters and son. Now grown up and moved out. Married with their own families and living far away. Duncan residing, north of Sidney, in Hunter Valley Australia but gratefully Paulette and Julianne only a couple of hour's drive away towards Gloucester.

Jenny wanted a new beginning. A place of her own. Easier to keep track of the heating bills than the four bedroomed home, big enough for her once family of five. The bungalow was only half a mile away from her home with Neville. A little closer to the city centre and still convenient for the local shops she had used her entire married life. She loved the bungalow and its closeness to the village just five minutes' walk away. The Mount Radford pub, at the cross roads next to the chemist and then the news agents. A small supermarket, the laundrette she never used and an art shop she never understood how it survived. And at the far end the jewellery shop where Neville had purchased her engagement and wedding rings so long ago, remembering the day he proposed on one knee like it was yesterday.

The city centre was only a short bus ride away. One appearing every half an hour, so she never had to worry about the time. It ran a circular route. Picking up from the village then into the city, dropping off right on the high street. It would make its way back via the swimming pool where Jenny was enrolled in an aqua fitness class each fortnight. It was less exercise and more chatting. Meeting up with old neighbours and friends who all now had fledged families of around the same age.

With one spare bedroom, Jenny had little room for her family when they came to visit. Paulette and Julianne normally arriving during the school holidays. Staying with old school friends still living in the area. A chance to relive old memories in the evenings, sharing a glass of wine while their kids shared the bedroom at Grandma's

Jenny loved taking her grandchildren to the swings nearby. Around the corner and down the hill to Bull Meadow Park play area and field. Below the old grounds of the hospital, now turned into the Barcelona Hotel. Occasionally they would take a longer walk into the town. Grandma always wanting to visit the toy shop along the high street and allow the grandchildren to choose a toy each. Paulette and Julianne always saying she shouldn't as the kids had plenty of toys at home.

She loved to spoil them. It was her treat when they came to visit.

Since leaving for Australia, Duncan had only returned once for the funeral of his father. His vineyard taking up all his time, not allowing him the freedom to visit as he wanted. Often phoning his mum. Always inviting her to stay but she made polite excuses unsure at her age if she could cope with the long flights and unsure who would look after Sasha.

"Good morning Andreas." Jenny announced in her jovial voice, arms out stretched to give him a hug as if he was a long-lost son.

"Good morning to you," Andreas responded, bending to wrap his arms around her and give her a hug she always insisted on.

There was plenty of affection in this lady's heart. It overflowed from an endless well of care and never-ending love expressed to one and all, especially to visitors to her home in her time as a caring mother, feeding any friends who arrived home with her son and daughters without a second thought laying a place at the table as if they were part of her family, sometimes feeding up to ten children in one sitting. She loved it, finding their youthful zest and hope in their fledgling lives uplifting, sad to see her family leave for university and then never properly return as they grew into adults and finally departed from her family home.

Outwardly Jenny enjoyed every day of her life but found living on her own lonely from time to time. She loved her activities each week, swimming and yoga class with the lovely bubbly Charlie, but the visit of Andreas was always a high point. To meet with someone younger, who was still engaged with life. Talented and good with his hands. And happy to entertain her and Sasha each fortnight

with a drive out to Riverside Valley Park allowing her
retired grey hound a chance to run wild.

Andreas could hear Sasha, shut into the kitchen of the
bungalow. She recognised his voice and what it meant.
Excited to sit in his van and take the short ride to the open
fields where she could run like her youth on the track and
enjoy open surroundings away from the hard pavements
and noise of the city.

"You ready then?" Andreas asked.

"Jacket and then Sasha and we are good to go." She
put a thumbs up to Andreas. The deep satisfying smile
showing her love of this man and the pleasure he brought
to her and her companion Sasha. He was the only
connection she had with the real world. Everything else was
in the bubble of retirement. The slower pace of life she did
not regret but always meeting with old people, did have its
draw backs.

Sat in Andreas's blue van, boots on her feet and a
navy-blue summer jacket around her shoulders Jenny
looked out the window grinning. Sasha was sat on the floor.
Held down by her lead, struggling to look out of the side
window. Tail sweeping back and forth showing her delight,
whimpering now and then with impatience. As the van
pulled into the gravel carpark Sasha's excitement could not
be contained. Desperate to get out and run.

"Steady girl." Jenny tried to calm her but it had no
effect. "Just you wait one more minute."

"I'll come round and take her. Don't want to see you
being dragged down the field at high speed." Andreas
jumped out and skipped around the front of the van

opening the passenger door slowly, reaching for the lead before Sasha took flight.

"Steady now, steady." Andreas looked at her, holding the lead tight and pressing down on her back legs to make her sit. Giving time for Jenny to get out and prepare herself for the walk.

"You're ever so good with her. A firm hand but kind. She enjoys your company, like I do."

"Thank you. I enjoy our walks together. It breaks up the weeks. Away from the sawdust and concrete of the job and I'm sure it does me as much good as Sasha."

"Well, I certainly benefit from it. I love our walks and chats. It's all very well being retired but I do love spending time around younger people. Someone still connected to the world outside retirement."

"I don't think I consider myself as young anymore. I'd save that for teenagers and people in their early twenties."

"You're only half way through. Take it from me, you are young. I hang around a few oldies during the week. Age seems to hit some folks really hard. And yet I've been lucky. Neville was a good age when he passed on. Don't you think?"

"I'm always astonished how active you keep yourself."

"No peace for the lazy in this world, my Neville used to say. You have to dig in and get on. He was right. Do you have enough work to keep you going?"

"Oh yes. I've built up a good reputation over the years. Do a good job, and people ask you back. And they tell other people. I've got customers waiting for me all over town. They say they would rather wait than call somebody else, who they don't know."

"I've mentioned you to a few of my friends. You did an unbelievable job on my kitchen."

"A lot of work reducing the height of the worktop by six inches but very rewarding."

"Couldn't live without my kitchen you know. Those few weeks when I first moved in. Having to keep moving the steps around. All the extra stretching I had to do. I was so glad when you finished the job."

"I'm very glad it meets with your approval."

"Shall we let Sasha off the lead?"

Andreas and Jenny had walked past the small brick building used as a changing room for the two football pitches. Sundays the busiest day. Families coming out and watching their children in the morning and then the dads playing afterwards. Today the pitches were empty, always the case on a Wednesday. No games taking place but a few children kicking a football about and a handful of walkers enjoying the August dry weather. Sasha was let off the lead and immediately ran off towards the end of the field.

"I love watching her run. She's a bit like me. Inside still twenty-one years old and thinking I can do all the things I used to," Jenny said watching Sasha run with her head down.

"Spring chicken." Andreas commented watching Sasha disappear.

"Bit of an old bird I think." Jenny replied smiling.

Andreas looked across at her cheerful smiling face. If you were asked to guess her age, you'd be wrong. She came across as a person much younger than her years. Still taking the greatest care in her dyed blond hair and ensuring a little make-up was applied each day. He found her beautiful. Always wondering if she would find another partner. When they spoke, she only ever mentioned the other ladies she visited and met with. Perhaps in life, some only have one love.

Sasha returned. Her run back much slower as age did not agree with her either. She sat in front of Jenny waiting for her treat, kept in a little bag in Jenny's coat pocket. Ensuring Sasha did not run off without returning.

"Can I ask you?" Andreas said.

"Anything," Jenny replied nodding to him.

"Would you ever have another relationship?"

"Oh, I think it's too late for me. And my family wouldn't like it."

"I think they are old enough to look after themselves. You shouldn't have to worry about them."

"Your children are always your children no matter what age they are. Their thoughts and opinions are always worth considering. I value what they think. Especially at my age. They don't call us oldies vulnerable for nothing."

"I've never thought of you as vulnerable."

"The world says we are but thank you. Having somebody younger around is a great help."

Jenny looked up at him and raised her eyebrows.

"The world can keep its silly views. I forget I am still a boy in my dad's eyes. Although we don't meet very much, him being in Scotland. It's a funny way of thinking."

"I don't know if I want to start dating at my age. Things change. Companionship becomes far more important than having another husband."

"Yes, I agree. We don't talk about the importance of being close to someone. More than a friend but not intimate in any way," Andreas replied.

"You talk as if you trying to convince yourself you are not lonely. I'm not sure if I was your age, I could be on my own as much as you."

"I have my work."

"Work's not enough." Jenny looked worryingly at him.

"And I keep busy in the little spare time I have. I do have a few friends."

"You never talk about them. Most men of your age are married with families. Spending their time down the pub watching football or something similar. You seem to spend far too much time on your own."

"I've never told you I have a motorbike, have I?"

"No, you haven't. Something I never wanted to be involved with. Far too dangerous."

"I go out on rides into the countryside and along the coast. I find it refreshing and exhilarating. I've been known to pack a few things and go off for the weekend. Went up to the Lake District on a weekend last year."

"But it's on your own."

"I meet up with a few other buddies."

"Ladies?"

"One or two," Andreas replied hesitantly.

"Anyone you can say you have a love for?"

"No not really. It's the riding I like."

"You never take a passenger?"

"No, just me."

"I don't understand you. Working and spending the occasional day with an old bird like me. You should be having the time of your life with a pretty young lady on your arm."

"It's not me," he replied.

"I won't push it. You seem very happy with life anyway. And I do love your company."

"I think I am. I make enough money to live a good life. Perhaps when the time is right, I'll meet someone and settle down."

"Glad to hear it. I loved every second of my marriage with Neville. He was such a gentleman. It's all different nowadays. Women seem to be more in control of things. Chivalry almost wiped off the face of the planet. I loved being taken care of by Nev'. Time to watch the kids grow up at home and not having to go out to work. You won't understand it but we home mums loved our lives.

Occasionally we wanted to give the kids away to someone else but overall, I did love it. They kept me young."

"And you still look young.," Andreas added.
Jenny shook her head. "There is a woman out there for you. Perhaps it would make life better. You won't know until you try."

She looked at him, putting her arm in his continuing to walk along the edge of the football field a short distance from the trees. Sasha darting off, disappearing into the trees but soon returning in the hope of another treat.

Andreas had never revealed his past to Jenny. Not on purpose. The only thing on his mind when they first met was getting the kitchen sorted out. It took all his energy to finish the job, being much more complex than he first thought. It gave him no time to chat or talk about his life. Day by day the past was left behind. Jenny doing the talking and Andreas listening with only a few words now and then helping the conversation along. She had presumed him single. He liked it. The lack of sympathy towards him refreshing.

After all he was single.

Over the weeks the job had taken, Andreas never offered any of his past. Not wanting the buoyant conversations to be interrupted by endless apologies and the sudden change in character people underwent as soon as they learned of his circumstance. They never said it but they felt sorry for him. With Jenny it was different.

"Have you ever thought about going to see Duncan?"

"Yes. And he keeps asking me when he phones. It's too far away."

"It would be a trip of a lifetime."

"I have a lifetime behind me. I don't think I can cope with the journey. I understand it takes days."

"Normally you stop off half way. I did a trip to Australia once and we flew to America for the stop over. Only a couple of hours. You could take a couple of days in America and make a mini vacation on the way."

135

"I couldn't do it on my own. Three or four days in a country I don't know. Maybe if I had a friend in the USA, it would be different but I've not been a great lover of overseas travel. Not without a husband to lead the way."

"What about one of your daughters taking you?"

"They would love to but their families keep their lives busy. There is no way either of them could afford the time away from their homes. Leaving them in the hands of their husbands. My goodness the mess." She shook her head. "I can't even begin to think of the fall out."

"I think you should go. It would do you good. A few months on the east coast, with its warm and sunny climate. Meeting up with Duncan and his family. Tasting the wine. Picking grapes. It would be fantastic."

"Perhaps you should go. Sounds like you would enjoy it."

"It's been a while since I've been abroad."

"Where did you go?"

"New Zealand then onto Sydney. North Sydney. It's on the other side of the Harbour Bridge looking across the water at the Opera house. Stayed a few days in a simple hotel before my friend drove us up north. I was younger then. With a carefree attitude, no money and a desire to see the world."

"What about New Zealand?"

"Spent a couple of days there as part of the same trip. It was such a blast."

"Well next time, I need to hear more about your adolescent adventures."

"Agreed," Andreas replied.

"Now, where's Sasha?"

Andreas pointed at her a little way in front.

"That's another disappointment about getting old. Eyesight. Why I drive so little any more."

"But you still have a car."

"I know. Can't bring myself to get rid of the old girl. And I like the occasional trip out with Sasha. All those memories tied up in her."

"It's a bit of a classic now."

"Like its owner."

"I disagree. You are still radiant and beautiful."

"Oh. Nobody's said anything so lovely for more than twenty years."

"What about Neville?"

"Although a gentleman he was not much with romantic words or gestures I'm afraid."

"That's no good. I've always thought you so active and uplifting from the very first time we met. When you tried to open your old front door and had to shout through the letter box."

"That was so funny. At least it proved the point it needed fixing but it had to wait. My kitchen came first. Any way you did fix it."

"Only temporarily."

"But it worked for another year. And you didn't charge me for it."

"It was only a five-minute job. I don't feel I have to charge for every second of my time. You paid me enough to do the kitchen."

"Worth every penny."

"Glad you're happy with it." Andreas replied.

"No, you. You are worth every penny."

"Oh, thank you. Do you have a ball in those magic pockets of yours?" Andreas asked.

"Yes, of course. Sasha's not very good at bringing it back. Likes the chase though."

"I won't throw it too far. I know she tires quickly."

"But she does love her time out. I can't give her the same energetic exercise around the town."

"I'm glad to help." Andreas replied throwing the ball.

"Perhaps you should have a dog. They are good companions."

"I spend too much time away from home. It wouldn't be fair."

"You know this thing with Duncan?" Jenny asked.

"Visiting him?"

"Yes."

"You've been thinking things over, haven't you?

"You know me. Still have a very active mind."

"What have you been thinking?"

"I'm not suggesting you do this by any stretch of the imagination but I want to ask."

"Go ahead."

"Would you come with me?"

There was silence. Only the sound of happy children in the distance and the panting of Sasha as she returned, without the ball, wanting another treat. Jenny fussed in her pocket and gave in to her tired looking face.

"There you go. Last one."

Sasha turned, now tired finding her place beside Jenny.

"What do you think?" Jenny asked looking up at Andreas.

"I don't know. It poses so many questions."

"Well give me an instant answer. Without any thoughts about all the reasons now going round in your head, telling you this is not a good idea."

"I'd love to, but."

"I know. There are a hundred and one things stopping it happening. It's the same for me. Who would look after Sasha? What would my family say? Me gallivanting off to the other side of the world with a younger man none of them know anything about?"

"Yes. What about my work? I don't know how I would be able to take a long time off without finding it difficult to pick things up afterwards. And the cost?"

"I wasn't expecting you to pay."

"You can't pay. That's not right."

"Why ever not?" Jenny replied with a little irritation.

Andreas furrowed his brow, stroking his beard.

"Because." He pondered on his answer.

"Yes?" Jenny replied looking at him and waiting for an excuse."

"Because I'm the guy who comes around to fix your house. Nothing to do with being family."

"Oh Andreas, you are much more than just a handyman. Surely you understand how important you are to me?"

He looked across at her. Never considering the impact of his visits to take Sasha out for a good walk. The loneliness he dissolved with a simple act.

"I'm not sure I've grasped how much my little visit means to you."

"Companionship Andreas. Your compliment today. I don't think you understand how wonderful it makes me feel to hear words like those. How it lifts me. Brings back memories of my youth and of my time with Neville."

"I didn't realise."

"You don't know how kind and caring you are. You have a big heart flowing with love for the people you meet and work for. You have so much you could offer another person. I don't understand why you aren't married with a lovely family? You'd make a perfect father."

Andreas took a deep breath. Trying with every fibre of his strength to hide his true and injured feelings.

"It's just not me." His reply artificially buoyant but hiding nothing.

Jenny looked at his face and for the first time could see something different in his expression. She knew what she was looking at. The faces at the funeral all looked the same.

"What is it you are not telling me?"

Andreas put his head down, continuing to walk slowly, now heading back towards the little building used as the changing room.

"It doesn't matter." He smiled at her on one side of this mouth. "It's time to take you and Sasha back home."

"Some sort of loss?" She asked, wanting to understand the look on his face.

"Another time perhaps," he replied politely. "I'm sorry I didn't mean to intrude. A bit of my mother hen coming back and sticking its nose in where it's not wanted. My three always said I wanted to know too much about their lives."

"Thank you anyway. For caring."

"Well, if you ever want to talk about it," she paused and tipped her head side to side, opening her hands in a relaxed gesture.

"I need to think about what you said earlier."

"Yes. Give it some thought. When you're back home. And let me know. Either way it doesn't matter."

"I will. I need a bit of time. For all the detail to sink in."

"Are you staying for lunch?"

"I can't today. I'm working a few miles away at Mrs Goodwin's, sorting out her garage door. She's having a new one fitted and I need to get it finished today."

"You know you're always welcome."

"It's appreciated. And it's always lovely of you to feed me."

"You wouldn't believe how difficult it is to shop for one. I don't think the food shops want to sell small amounts of anything."

"Perhaps you should invite your ladies around now and then?"

Jenny didn't like the idea. Happy to meet outside her home but not fill her house with more old people. She pursed her lips.

"I don't think so. Well, you need to get me back to Rectory Bungalow and get off and finish a garage door."

"Yes. Back to work. Half day over. Customers waiting. Wouldn't do to upset them, would it?"

Andreas drove down the short road to Rectory Bungalow and turned the van around for a quick exit. Sasha was happy to be home. Less enthusiastic now after her long run and walk not needing restraining as she jumped down to the ground and waited for Jenny. Andreas put a hand out to help Jenny down from the seat.

"Thank you, young man."

"My pleasure."

"Two weeks?" she asked hopefully.

"All being well, I'll be back here at the same time."

"Good. Give me a shout if you can't make it. No point you turning down work to take an old biddy and her dog for a walk."

"I like our Wednesdays. A breather for the week. Perhaps next time we should go somewhere different?"

"Yes. If it's not too much bother. You think of somewhere and surprise me. I'd like that."

Jenny held out her arms to give Andreas a goodbye hug.

"Take care. See you soon," she said hopefully.

She reached up and put her hands on his cheeks, drawing him down and kissing him on the forehead. Understanding there was something in his life buried deep out of sight he was hiding. She missed him already and he hadn't even driven off. She knew it was silly but his company meant so much to her. And Sasha always enjoyed their time together.

He straightened up and walked back to the driver's side of the van opening the door, ready to go. Today not wanting to say any more but to get back to work, putting his head down and pushing any of the thoughts about Australia or Jenny's delving question to sleep for a while.

Sharing his sad past with her was something he never wanted to do. Always loving his chance to be single without having to carry all the emotional luggage permanently resting on his shoulders. He knew it would change. Sympathy washing into their friendship and changing it forever, Jenny undoubtedly would behave in a different way. It would spoil things. But then this offer of going to Australia with her. It was out of the question. Full of pitfalls like her family. How would they feel about this stranger going off with their mother? It was enough to put him off. He imagined Paulette and Julianne seeing him as a money grabber. Syphoning off her money and being labelled as someone very undesirable for their old mum.

The offer had a magnetism. Pulling him back to the question over and over again.

He needed to get the garage door finished.

***

(Chapter 2, from my book 'Restoration'.)

33.
'A Change in the Light'

Cynthea Gregory

Eleven, Eleven, Eleven.

That morning, the street in our story started quietly. It was waiting. The brick-built terraced homes stared at each other in anticipation across the road. Long rectangular windows glared at their carbon copies opposite. Strong cold gusts of wind blew between them, rattling them in their wooden frames. The wings of a crow hung on it against the flat greyed sky. It blew over someone's muddy bicycle. It ruffled the hair of a boy, clutching a precious loaf of bread, as he strode homewards. It bit at his fingers, at his knees, exposed beneath his woolly school uniform, tingeing them red. Head down, he progressed past each of the tiny front yards. Past all of the short paths leading from that Birmingham pavement, all ending at identical front doors.

The boy stopped. His head came up, listening. He squinted towards the end of row of houses. There were voices. Loud voices. It was starting. The performance of that November day. After only seconds, he took on board what he was before him. Breakfast forgotten, he broke into a sprint, wanting a closer look. A lorry advanced, at a snails' pace because of its cargo. The human load filled the back, clung to the sides, even sat on top of the cab. The rattling and juddering of the lorry was obliterated by the shouting, singing and cheering coming from it. The men's voices shattered the morning's calm. Their fracas brought faces to windows. Front doors were wrenched open. Coats are quickly pulled on. Buttoned up. Our boy with the bread yelled something to a man hanging onto the vehicle. The boy was beckoned, and then was lost amidst the growing crowd following on behind.

Inside number twenty two, a small hand wiped the mist of condensation from the front room window. Teresa lifted the half curtain, clearing their view. Over the space of the front yard, they studied the applauding throng.

'Is it really finished Terry?' the owner of the smaller hand asked.

'You know it is. They'll all be going to the park to celebrate.'

'And she'll go soon?' Kate whispered into the window.

'Well, she'll have to. Once Pa returns, she'll have to go, won't she?' Teresa said. 'There'll be no room, with only two bedrooms.' Teresa's face contorted as she imitated a mystical creature breathing fire, 'h-a-a-a-a-h, no room for fierce, smoke-breathing dragons.'
Her sister's face relaxed. Her hand went out to Teresa. They giggled quietly, privately. Kate responded to a wave from someone following the wagon filled with its live freight.

'Come and eat breakfast,' their mother shouted.

'But Ma, come and see,' Kate called towards the kitchen.

'Kate, come out of the front parlour,' her mother's voice had become higher, sharper. The sisters surveyed one another. Teresa's mouth pursed. She brought a warning finger before it.

Several seconds silence passed, before the command came again, 'Come here now. And you, Terry.'
They slid their stockinged feet slowly over the cold tiles of the front entrance and ambled towards the kitchen door. The warmth from the range washed over them as they stepped inside. Ma stood beside the table, cutting rationed bread. Four very slim slices dropped onto the bread board. A saucer containing a meagre portion of margarine sat beside it.

'Hurry up you two, you need to get to school,'
'But Ma everybody's going…..' Teresa argued as she pulled a chair away from the table.

'That's where you're wrong Terry, not everybody's going to the Armistice celebrations. It's Monday, and you are both going to school; and I'm going to work.'
Teresa wasn't satisfied, 'But Ma, it's an important day. There'll never be another one.' Kate listened to the exchange, her eyes darting between her sister and her mother. Without a word, she shoved pieces of bread and marg into her mouth. Being three years her sister's junior, she hasn't yet learnt the art of challenging adults.

'Don't you argue with me young lady,' Ma snapped, pointing an index finger towards her elder daughter. 'We are not going to celebrate something that took your Pa away from us for years, killed Aunty Dorothy's husband, your cousin and nine million other soldiers. Do your sister's hair, then get your boots on.'

Teresa being Teresa wanted to continue the altercation, 'But, they're not rejoicing 'cos all the soldiers died, it's 'cos the war is all over and no more'll die.' She scraped her chair back across the tiles. She realised the next comment would prompt a reaction, but she said it anyway. 'And Dorothy's husband died from the 'flu, didn't he, Ma?'

Ma leaned forward in order to cuff Teresa across the head. A loud tut escaped her.

'You horrible child! It's Aunty Dorothy to you my girl.'

Ma tidied her hair in front of the only mirror in the house, forcing a dark felt hat over it. A large shiny hat pin was skewered through the back.

Teresa's mouth turned down as she edged around her mother in search of the hairbrush. It was snatched up from the mass of clutter on the sideboard. Terry was riled: irked that she had to call that woman aunty. Dorothy, who was already at work. Dorothy, who wasn't an aunt at all. Dorothy who was just their lodger. Someone that mother had met at Phillips — the factory where they both worked — Dorothy in the offices, Ma on the assembly line.

Women's Rights had brought them together. After work, they'd attended meetings; took part in marches. Or the two women went from house to house, collecting signatures. They handed out pamphlets. At first, the girls had been involved. But, when the children experienced the hostility against them, Ma decided it was not right that they should be there. They'd been heckled. Shouted at. Sworn at. Had doors slammed in their faces. Egg yolk had splattered their clothing. Hence Teresa and Kate remained at home, looking after themselves. They huddled next to the range. Reading time after time from the few books they had. They made-up stories. Played games. Whispered and mumbled about Dorothy, and how they detested her.

One day Dorothy had received a telegram stating that her husband had died. He'd been amongst the first victims of the Spanish influenza pandemic, whilst serving in France. Soon afterwards, Teresa opened the door to Dorothy. She stood on their doorstep, laden with some of her belongings. She'd come to live with them.

Within days, the lodger transformed the children's lives. The atmosphere at number twenty two changed dramatically. The ring of childish laughter faded away. Their songs were sung away from home. Ma no longer joined in their puerile games. No more bedside stories by lamplight. No words of reassurance that their father would hopefully return soon. There was no warmth from her arms around their slight forms. Ma's warmth was transferred to Dorothy. She became most important inhabitant at number twenty two. She dominated their mother's time. What she wanted happened. The women shared smiles. The girls were excluded from these; and many of their conversations.

Dorothy wasn't used to living with children. She treated them as a great inconvenience, or as skivvies to do jobs for her. Within hours, both the girls regretted her becoming part of the household. Within days, they loathed the sight of Aunty Dorothy. She'd stolen the joy of youth from them. In bed, Teresa and Kate clung to each other, muttering under the bed clothes. Wondering. Trying to reason how one spiteful, loud-mouthed stranger had stolen their mother away.

Ma let in a draught of cold air as she opened the back door. She left to use the outside privy. Kate took this opportunity to imitate Teresa's performance of a dragon, which she'd obviously found amusing.

'H-a-a-a-h, fire and flames,' she laughed, acting out her version of Dotty Dragon, 'h-a-a-a-h.'

That was the nickname they had given her. They thought it suited her large personality; her vicious temperament. She had the breath of a dragon, which puffed out rings of smoke, as she exhaled from her cigarettes.

Teresa hushed her. 'Shh, you'll be in trouble if Ma hears you.'

Teresa started to pull the brush through Kate's long caramel coloured hair: pulling out the tangles, brushing it down her back. As Teresa was tying butterfly bows each side of it, Ma returned.

Kate's head tilted, 'Listen.'

They all heard a thundering. A rumble which shook the house. Another vehicle rolled past, slowly heading for the park.

Kate went to stand up.

'You, stop wasting time. Get to school,' Ma bawled as she headed for the door.

'Ma, now the war's over, what will happen when Pa comes home?' Kate asked the question that was upper-most in her mind.

'I ain't got time to talk about that now,' Ma said sourly, 'I'll be late for work. Get yourselves to school.'

Then she was gone, the door slamming behind her. Kate's pale face dropped.

'You know you were wasting your time asking now,' Teresa said.

Minutes later, they exited the protection of their home. They followed the path of their mother towards the pavement. Kate jerked her sister's hand to turn left at the wall — towards the school, towards Phillip's factory. Their arms stretched out. Teresa, determined, tugged in the opposite direction. Turning right: following the few pedestrians heading up the road.

'Come on Kate. We're going to the park to see what's happening.'

'What if Ma finds out?'

'She won't. School can wait for an hour or two.'

'You'll get a thrashing.'

'Fine, you go to school by yourself. I'm going to the park.'

As Teresa suspected, Kate did not let go of her hand. Her fingers clung on even tighter. She'd worked out that Kate would feel like her. It was worth taking the chance of a beating to find out what was happening. Teresa strode confidently past the terrace of houses, pushing against the force of the cold, dragging her sister in her haste. The icy wind quickly pierced through their poor quality coats. It tangled Kate's hair which she had been so lovingly brushed. Within seconds, sounds from the park guided them. Initially, they heard the thud of music. As they neared, they distinguished the instruments of a brass band. The commotion of many voices. Singing. Shouting in unison.

Teresa broke into a run, her spirits rising. Her little sister had no choice, but to follow suit. They cast off the sensation of cold. But the scene the other side of the park railings brought them to a halt. There were more people gathered than they'd ever experienced before. Before them was a mass of passions. An eruption of rejoicing. A palette of uniforms. Olive, khaki, navy and flashes of red, white and blue. Men in great coats. Women wearing their working clothes. Women in their best. Lorries, buses and a smattering of cars parked haphazardly. They neared the gated entrance in silence. Overawed, they dared not move. But Teresa felt eager to join in with the singing, the dancing, the arms draped over shoulders, the multitude of smiles. She longed to help wave the flags. She just needed to find a little courage.

Out of the blue, Kate let go of her hand. Teresa turned to see her sister being whirled around in the air. A bright and cheerful young man had grabbed her from behind. Her thin legs swung upwards and outwards.

'Out the way, mi duck,' he grinned, before placing Kate carefully inside the park. She giggled.

'You be good girls now, ta-ra,' he raised his trilby towards them. He parted waving. Then he was engulfed by the crowds. Kate waved at his back; returned his grin. Trepidation hindered her progress, but seizing hold of Kate's hand again improved her level of determination. She surveyed the alien circus of jubilation around them. She needed to take control.

'Don't go wandering off now,' she instructed, 'I'd never find you again amongst this lot. Let's go and see the band.'

Teresa kept to the edge of the hordes, and heading towards the sound of brass instruments, Kate in tow.

34.
Færie Ointment

Sim Taylor

'Why can't you see in one of your eyes?' Ellen asked Bridget.

Ellen was ten years old and sitting in a picturesque cottage garden with her own mother and their neighbour, Bridget. Ellen, who was an inquisitive girl liked to spend time at Bridget's cottage because the tiny cottage with its jars and books in every corner and things piled up everywhere was so interesting and different from her own home where things were spick and span and in Ellen's opinion very boring. The child's mother, Anita - nudged her daughter leaning over and whispering in Ellen's ear, 'That is a personal question and it is not polite to ask personal questions.'

Bridget winked at Ellen as she told her 'Now that is a very long story and there is not enough time today to tell it.'

Bridget lived on her own and had done so for some time whether from widowhood or from choice nobody could remember a time when there had been another living in the cottage with the old woman. Bridget didn't have any children of her own that would listen to her stories but she felt in her bones that Ellen, perhaps in a few years time, would be the woman to whom she could pass on some of stories to. Bridget hoped that this would be the case because otherwise her knowledge of local legends would be lost forever. The art of storytelling had decreased dramatically in recent years and seemed to be decreasing at an ever faster rate and inversely proportional to the number of cars and televisions in the village. Bridget considered that like each generation before her the older women and indeed the men of the village lamented the past and grumbled about how the changes that were taking place were going to be detrimental to all - 'You mark my words' the old would mumble knowingly to the young in the local pub over a pint of local cider with the wood crackling on the fire in the hearth. The young would laugh later but deep down, especially in the wiser young people, there would be a jolt or a tingle in their bones which would make them think that perhaps the older folk in the village did have a point and that life was just rushing past now with little time to listen to the tales and the wisdom of the older folk of the village. They had little time for those who had lived there all their lives and had time to talk and think.

Bridget's small stone cottage was dark with only tiny windows inside, one of the defining features were the bunches of drying herbs. The purple, grey and blue bunches hung from the ceiling beams and their fragrance brought a soothing peace to her home. Her pantry contained dried wild plants useful for her work as a natural healer. Bridget had tiny sealed jars of dried fungi and she was known to be an expert fungi forager. Everyone in the village could identify the main species that were good to eat without causing sickness. Bridget however was able to go way beyond the basics to know which fungi held properties that would help with healing. She knew which specimens held the necessary nutrients that could help a woman in labour or to lift someone who was suffering from depression after the birth. She knew which tinctures would soothe a swollen stomach or calm a sore head. Some in her village called her a nurse. Although she dismissed this as she lacked formal training in a hospital, neither had she gone to college to learn her craft. Instead, she had learnt how to make tinctures and balms from her mother and from her mother's mother.

The women in the nearby village respected Bridget's knowledge and trusted her remedies. Bridget was not complacent. She knew that the trust of the village women took years or generations even to accomplish. Out here on the edge of the moor in the 1960s and 1970s she was all they had. Fortunately she had been good at her healing so long as the essential ingredients were available. They had reason to trust her skills as they had been cured of various maladies and indeed it had been Bridget who had supported them as they birthed their children and treated them in the aftermath with kindness when their milk failed to flow or they suffered with mastitis. No one knew for sure whether Bridget had ever birthed any children of their own but it was without question that Bridget had knowledge of childbirth and they trusted in her to give each woman confidence in the ability of her own body to do the work of giving birth. Bridget was also respected as someone who had saved the life of many a baby or mother in childbirth. In exchange, they would bring whatever they could to help Bridget. They were very generous with their gifts, although they could see that Bridget lacked nothing in her life. Her stove was always warm and delicious aromas greeted them whenever they visited. Bridget didn't need their company. She wasn't lonely but she loved to have visitors and warmly welcomed the younger women with sweet treats and honeyed exotic teas that didn't fail to refresh them in spirit and energy. It was almost magical how rejuvenated they felt after a visit filled with laughter and stories whilst sitting outside Bridget's cottage in the spring or summer sunshine.

Bridget's home was never tidy but there was a place for everything. Every nook and cranny had something of significance. Whether a charm or an ornament that was useful in the ceremonies that Bridget used to bring about healing. Spiders' webs were not brushed away but instead they were a welcome addition to the ceilings.

In its turn, the garden was not manicured but instead everything in it was useful and either beautiful or functional (often both). Each plant had a purpose whether to be eaten or of good medicinal properties. Some plants were good for insects or bees by attracting the pollinators. Bridget cherished and held these plants in high esteem. Birds, insects and animals were protected and encouraged in the space. Birds sang in the trees and shrubs around the garden. Bridget would greet each creature each morning and in turn was rewarded with a song or the lifting of spirit that its presence in her life brought.

Bridget's cottage was on the very edge of the village. It suited Bridget to be both on the edge of the wild moors and also to be so close to the woodlands - for it was there where her foraging took place. She spent her days more outside than in. Bridget valued the importance of her knowledge and the knowledge of the plants and wildlife close to her on the edge of Dartmoor where she had lived all her life. She knew the exact spot where a plant or fungi she needed could be found. She nurtured the plants that provided for her and thanked mother nature with offerings and by respecting the earth. She knew not to take too much or not to take anything at certain times of the year. She understood the ecology and the relationships with the soil, water and trees to create the right conditions for the plant that she needed. Whether it was rose hips or sorrel, feverfew or willow - she trod carefully on the earth. Each step measured, gracious and humble. She would listen to the sounds around her - her fellow creatures. She spoke to the animals around her. The robins and starlings, her favourites, would alight on her bony hands, wrinkled and brown from years of exposure to the elements.

Bridget, living in Devon and the edge of Dartmoor, was more than familiar with the existence of pixies. Tales of Dartmoor pixies abound. She enjoyed retelling the myths and legends of Dartmoor that own mother had passed to her as a child. She enjoyed the different layers to the stories of the moor. There was the superficial story that a child enjoyed and then there was the deeper meaning that only those who really tuned in would understand. Finally, there were those who truly believed in the creatures and tales of the moor. Those who respected that there were things that seemed out of this world but that there was always an element of truth in the tales of old. It took courage to move between worlds and then it was important to only confide in others who were believers or the rumours would begin and untold damage was usually the result of a careless tongue. For example, some locals in the village spoke of Bridget and her many heavy cloth bags - payment for services they said. Others knew that there was little chance of Bridget being paid for her services in silver as most folks didn't have much money. Except for rich folk that is and they wouldn't want the services of a village herbal healer without training now. So the tales of Bridget's money bags were little more than just tales. In fact, it had been a few years since Bridget's services as a midwife had been required. Car transport meant that the birthplaces of the youngest generation were no longer their mothers' cosy bedrooms but instead the harsh cold lights of a hospital in Exeter or Plymouth. But one night Bridget's services were required again and this is the story of that time.

One fearful stormy night, in the darkest depths of January, Bridget had taken to her bed early as it was so dark and cold in the cottage. A thunderstorm could be something to behold in these parts and there was torrential rain as most folks had never seen before. Sensible folks do not venture out onto the moor in such weather so Bridget was surprised to hear a banging at her cottage door. She expected to find a fallen branch knocking against the door when she got up and ventured to the door accompanied by a flash of lightning so bright that it lit the small hallway. Instead she could see a handsome black horse silhouetted against the sky and aboard the great horse was a very small man and it was he who had been knocking at her door with a large stick. Not many men of wealth visited Bridget so she was very interested to hear what this fine gentleman glad in a heavy but finely-made purple coat would have to say.

The man was polite and was looking for help from Bridget. 'Please, I need you to help me with my wife - she needs a midwife' he pleaded with Bridget to come with him. His voice was otherworldly and Bridget suspected that he was of the underworld and in all likelihood a real pixie. She had heard many tales from others of the pixie folk but had never been fortunate enough to meet one. She was excited but also slightly fearful of the pixie folk as not all the tales ended well for the human folk who met with their pixie brethren.

Bridget called out above the noise of the wind that it would have to wait until the passing of the storm as it was too dangerous to cross the river on such a night as this. 'It is a murderous night out there tonight' she told the small man. She urged him to call back or tell her the problem so she could give him the correct remedy for his wife.

His response was persistent with promises of a large sum of money. His wife was in labour and in pain and she needed a midwife and he would not be leaving without her. Bridget was not greedy but was tempted by the sum offered and was thinking how this amount would help to support her in her old age which was a topic on her mind frequently of late. But a woman in labour, she couldn't ignore even on a terrible night such as that night. Her principles meant she would not accept money for this. It was not right to do so in her opinion. She agreed to go with the man once she had gathered some of her potions and had dressed herself appropriately for facing the storm. Indeed the man was truly honourable and helped her onto his horse and produced a magnificent cloak that was warm as well as waterproof so Bridget did not suffer as she rode with the man back to his home.

The wind and cold rain lashed her face as they travelled together on the horse. Bridget held firmly to the man who was sitting in front of her astride the saddle. She could feel the warmth from the quality of the cloak for it was one of the coldest nights that Bridget could remember. In the dark, Bridget could not see where they were going. She was glad that she had brought her own handmade mittens made from gathered fleece. If she had not had these her hands would have surely frozen, she thought.

The man had made Bridget promise that she would not speak of anything that she saw or heard during that evening or a bad omen would befall her. This made Bridget even more convinced that this man was indeed a pixie. Her fear mixed with a sense of deep privilege that this man had come to her for help. Fewer men nowadays called on a healer. She wondered how he and his wife had come to hear about her healing power. Bridget also had no desire to antagonise the spirits and in fact she was wise enough to think that there were lots of things in this world that she did not fully understand and that this experience would be another such tale that would be too difficult to explain to others.

When the man finally stopped the horse it startled Bridget and she supposed that somehow she had fallen into a sleep despite the uncomfortable position. She saw a small house that seemed to Bridget to be magical and of another world. Bridget thought to herself that it was as though they had passed through a magic portal from the dark world of her own cottage on a stormy night to the idyllic world of the pixie world. The pixie cottage was a perfect but tiny cottage in a delightful woodland. In Bridget's mind's eye the only thing that Bridget could compare it to was the most perfect cottage in the Snow White tale. It was thatched with a golden straw and the tiny windows were clean and sparkling in the sun. The cottage was painted a pink colour like candy floss and tiny red velvety roses wound their way around the frame of the tiny blue painted door to the cottage. It was bathed in a light like that of a summer's eve. The scent of the roses was also pleasant and it conjured up an image that made Bridget question whether she was in a dream. She pinched herself to check and recalled tales of pixie folk that were between this world and the world of spiritual realms not understood on this earth except by mystics who could bridge between the two worlds.

Bridget ducked her head and entered the tiny hallway where stunning silver lamps lit the corridor. The lamps spoke of immense wealth in any realm whether human or supernatural. Bridget could hear a woman groaning the familiar pain of childbirth. Bridget hurried toward the sounds and entered a sumptuous bedroom. Bridget had to bow to get through the doorway and within was a perfect bed of reduced size not much bigger than a doll's bed. On it a beautiful perfect young woman was grimacing in the early stages of her labour. Her hair was silver and shining. Bridget couldn't help but believe that this woman was a faerie princess. Her skin though rosy through the pain of childbirth was translucent and perfect like that of a doll.

Bridget worked out that despite riding seemingly for hours that the time that had elapsed for the faerie woman was but a few moments of waiting for her husband to return with Bridget.

Bridget prepared ointments that would help soothe the pains and soon the woman's labour was much relieved. Bridget, although busy, had a chance once or twice to glance out of the window of the room and onto a picture of paradise. It was as the garden of Eden, and Bridget although surprised, was not too perplexed as generations of tales handed down to her about pixies made her feel strangely familiar with the tiny family and their world. She was elated to have been chosen to help the birth of this pixie family - she felt a feeling of wellbeing that it was almost as though she was drunk on the perfume and fortune of this perfect family.

Towards dawn the tiniest and loveliest of babies was born. The baby boy was adored by both parents immediately and Bridget was asked to apply ointment given to her by the husband from a tiny blue faerie ointment jar. The jar was no larger than Bridget's tip of her thumb. The ointment had to be placed on the baby's eyelids. This Bridget did. But without thinking, somehow the faerie box ended up in Bridget's potions box and was forgotten about with all the excitement of the baby's birth.

Bridget stayed in the cottage whilst the mother, Ellie recovered and the baby boy who they named Briden after Bridget grew stronger. Ellie told Bridget many tales of her life as a faerie princess. She showed her the perfect land in which they lived. She told her how it was only accessible only through the portal deep within the bogs of the moor. It was essential for the journey to the portal, that it was dark and raining to make the transition between the world - water was essential for the passage of mortals to the faerie world.

Bridget had to sit on the floor as she listened because the furniture in the house, although robust and well built, was too small for her human physique. The family said that in the faerie world outside of the house there was great beauty without frost or snow and not chill winds to bring hardship or sickness. Bridget recognised many of the plants but there were some that were new to her. The Pixie Prince, Grippli warned her that the plants should not be picked as the return through the portal would destroy the magic properties and instead turn to poison. Bridget was wise enough to heed the advice. The family gave Bridget many tiny gifts including a tiny grinder that the pixie folk used to create their own balms and potions from the pixie plants.

Grippli told Bridget that in the Otherworld everyone was horrified by the ways in which humans destroyed everything they touched with their greed and how most of the humans had little respect for nature. He warned Bridget that no good would come to humans who were hell bent on destruction. He went on to tell her that this was why he had come to Bridget for help as he knew that she believed in Pixies and she was kind to all creatures and plants of the Earth.

At the end of the week, Grippli brought his black horse to the front door to take Bridget back to her cottage on the edge of the moor. This time Grippli covered

Bridget's eyes with a brightly-coloured silk scarf before crossing the boundary between the faerie world and the human world.

Bridget was amazed that on her return to the cottage that she had not been away for more than a day. The only reminders were the tiny gifts including the silk scarf and the tiny grinder Bridget kept amongst the tiny knick knacks in a corner of her home. Later, the tiny objects solidified the story to those she confided in as there was no doubt that the workmanship was not of the human world. Bridget wore the silk scarf each day as a reminder of the Faerie World. She was in awe of the world that she had experienced and it was a while before she returned to her normal routine. She had found at first that she even missed the tiny family that she had grown so fond of when she had spent time with them. She often thought back to their kindness and the respect which they gave her. Real respect and trust was rare today in Bridget's opinion. After the visit to the Other World, Bridget found that she noticed things differently. She was more observant of the animals and birds around her. She listened more and started to care even more for the local environment. In a small way she wanted to create a perfect Pixie World where all were kind and respectful to each other whether they were human, plant or animal.

Bridget would swear now that she understood the song of the birds and the message that the bees buzzed. It enlightened her life but it was not something that she shared with others. She knew where the boundaries lay. It was as if this talent was also a curse. Perhaps this was the curse of the Pixies. Bridget believed that there was in fact always a price to pay for a journey to the Other World.

In fact, it was several months before Bridget found the faerie ointment box in her potions box. She felt a pang of guilt that she had inadvertently taken the ointment. She touched its beautiful enamelled top and at first she was not tempted to test out the magic potion. She resolved to find a way to get the ointment back to its rightful owner.

However, one day her temptation got the better of her and she decided to try out the ointment on one of her own eyelids. Bridget put a tiny amount on her right eyelid. It seems to have no immediate effect but the next morning Bridget found that the world through her right eye was different and everything appeared huge even Bridget's own cat was as large as a wild cat. But if she closed her right eye her left eye had normal vision.

Later that day, there was a knock at her door and Bridget was not surprised to see that outside there was the black horse that belonged to Grippli. Bridget was surprised that the Grippli appeared to be of normal stature but she knew why he was there and in a short time she handed over the faerie ointment jar.

Grippli, although put out by the loss of the ointment, gave Bridget another payment of gold coins as a gift from Ellie who was grateful to Bridget for the care she had given her. This was the last time that Bridget ever saw Grippli, Ellie or the baby pixie. Although she didn't forget her adventure as from that day her eyesight in the right eye was forever changed to darkness. Bridget turned to Ellen and smiled. It had taken 20 years to tell Ellen the real reason why she could only see in one eye.

Ellen was listening intently to Bridget's tale and smiled at the memory of asking the question all those years before. Ellen examined the gifts that Bridget had received from her visit to the pixie family and which Bridget kept in her cottage. Bridget watched the young woman's face as she took in everything she was told. It was an exercise in trust but Ellen had already put her trust in Bridget as together they had healed the most important person in Ellen's world. Ellen and Bridget met frequently these days since Ellen had moved back to Dartmoor after University and when Anita had fallen ill and needed some nursing care. Ellen had always been interested in alternative therapies but she had read most of what she knew from books and it wasn't until she began to talk to Bridget about some of the therapies that she was using with Anita that a whole new world opened up to her. Bridget had helped Ellen to prepare remedies to help Anita, all made from natural and local ingredients from scratch. There was no need to buy expensive ingredients in phials from the shops of Totnes or London as Bridget knew how to prepare the ingredients using local plants and herbs from her own garden using the faerie grinder. Bridget now used the grinder every day in her healing medicines. It seemed to Bridget that this grinder was the very best and that the balms and potions were more potent than the ones that she made before her visit to the underworld of the pixie world. Bridget explained how the potions and balms from local plants were the best to treat a person living in the local environment. Just as a person living in Yorkshire would be best treated by the plants of

Yorkshire so the same applied to Dartmoor. The more local the ingredients the better the remedy Bridget reassured Ellen.

Ellen's eyes had opened further to the beautiful garden of her childhood full of birds, insects and small animals. What Ellen hadn't realised though was that every plant in the small cottage garden had a purpose - some had been grown by Bridget and others - wild plants or weeds were encouraged to make their home in her garden. Bridget helped Ellen to understand that there was no such thing as weeds. Ellen and Bridget spent time together in the evenings - Ellen even learnt to spin and knit with Bridget. During these times Ellen had listened to stories of the village and beyond - stories about mermaids and the pixies of Dartmoor. To begin with Ellen believed that all the stories were make believe and passed down by word of mouth so that even if there had been an element of truth the truth was so distorted that the tale was now very much a work of fiction. But recently, Ellen was finding that she was wondering whether the tales were indeed true and that it was just that the listener had to be tuned into the world in a different way to see that there were messages in each tale that taught her something about the world. She was learning that there was very much a lot to learn from these tales and the women who told them.

**

In this telling of the Faerie Ointment the main character is depicted as a wise woman of the woods rather than as a wayward woman or witch. This is to redress the fact that many folk tales do not reflect well on women and especially older women. If you visit Dartmoor you will find many homes have figures of pixies in the garden. Some people call them gnomes. Throughout the county there are many tales of encounters with pixie folk and in the small East Devon town of Ottery St Mary there is an annual Pixie Day. The children of the town dress up as pixies and re-enact an encounter with pixies on mid-summer's night. A tradition that is part of the folklore of the town still today.

35.
Sorry For Any Inconvenience

Philip Algar

"I really can't understand where it is. It's just vanished."

Sheila was accustomed to her husband Tony announcing items that had disappeared but she could hardly ignore the latest outburst which was delivered with a combination of anger, frustration and a touch of panic.

"So what have the mischievous and invisible aliens done now?"

She realised from his angry growl that, whatever was missing it was important and jesting was ill-advised.

"It's my passport and if I don't find it soon my trip to San Francisco will be off. You used to keep all our important documents. Can you remember where you put it?"

Like politicians, her husband was anxious to place the blame on someone else. Sheila, who could be embarrassingly and, occasionally deliberately naïve, suggested that if he explained what had happened, the Americans would let him in because his name would be on their records. Tony puffed in indignation and pointed out that the world's leading tennis player, Jock O'Vitch, as he called him, was denied entry to the United States because he had not been vaccinated against Covid, so "I don't think that they'll let me in. Anyway, it must be found and quickly because otherwise I shall miss my train to Woking and then the coach to Heathrow. "

"Yes, dear, I know that but your plane doesn't take off until 9.00 this evening and I'm sure that it'll soon turn up. Now, in the first half of the winter, you re-organised every piece of paper in the house." She refrained from pointing out that the second half of the winter had been dominated by looking for documents that had hitherto always been located with the minimum of fuss.

"So, let's see your list of box files and their contents."

Meekly, he handed her the sheet and she was surprised to see that a passport might be included in a number of boxes. The list included:

OFFICIAL DOCUMENTS,
MISCELLANEOUS DOCUMENTS
AWAITING FILING,
AWAITING ASSESSMENT,
TRAVEL-OVERSEAS,
TRAVEL DOMESTIC,
GOVERNMENT-ISSUED DOCUMENTS
  and
DOCUMENTS AWAITING RENEWAL.

Showing a remarkable degree of self-control, she asked which of the eight box files he had searched. Apparently, he had not looked at any, forgetting that a new system was in force, and had only looked four times in a desk drawer, which had been the former home of the missing passport. Sheila supressed a snort and suggested that they look in turn at the collection of box files. She opted for two of the more likely containers and her frustrated husband opted for the less plausible TRAVEL-OVERSEAS and MISCELLANEOUS DOCUMENTS. Sheila was confident but after an hour nothing had emerged and Tony was becoming very annoyed. His wife, too, was irritated by his repeated assertion that the passport would appear in the last place that they searched. She explained that that was obvious, "as I've explained many times during the last few weeks".

After a further crucial 90 minutes Sheila wondered if the passport had slipped to the floor of the desk under the bottom draw. She was right but Tony, who grunted gratitude, was not as happy as might have been expected.

"My flight takes off at 9.00 this evening and I have to check-in three hours before. Then I've got to reach Woking in time to take the hourly coach service to Heathrow. That doesn't leave too much time if anything else goes wrong. I think my best bet is to forget lunch."

"You've plenty of time, it's only just 12.00 now, but I'll make you some sandwiches that you can eat on the train. Anyway, you've packed and I presume that you have your ticket and ESTA form?"

"Thanks. I'm sure I'm worrying unnecessarily but I've always worked on the assumption that if anything can go wrong, it will. That's a fundamental rule that you learn as you get older."

Tony was doubtless surprised that the journey to the local station was without incident. He would not have been surprised if a flock of sheep or several broken-down tractors and trailers had blocked their route. That said, such problems had beset him in the past. Even more surprisingly, the train, the one he had always intended to catch, was on time which meant that the remainder of his journey to Heathrow should fit in precisely with his schedule, which, he admitted to himself, was generous and should ensure that he would be in time to be on board his transatlantic flight.

As he settled into a seat in a nearly empty carriage, and began to munch his sandwiches, he allowed himself to ponder the potential outcome of his visit to Head Office in San Francisco. It was not entirely clear why he had been invited to meet some senior personnel but, he reasoned, they would not be summoning him, by first class, if he was to be demoted or, worse still, fired. He had tried to find out why he had to go to San Francisco but a wall of puzzling silence greeted his questions which was worrying. He was also concerned that, according to some of his friends who had ventured abroad on holidays, that the passenger now had to do most of the checking-in and other procedures by himself via computers. This was disconcerting because computers had hated Tony since the early days, when he had spoken to one in harsh terms. They continued to impose problems and it was probable that those based in the airport had been alerted.

His attention switched from California to Devon as he gazed at the passing scenery. Yes, he was lucky to live in such an attractive part of England and he wondered, what would his reaction be if he was to be promoted and had to live in San Francisco. For that matter, how would Sheila react, not least as many of her relatives lived in the area and she was an active member of a number of local clubs? Tony himself had few such connections, having become a workaholic some years ago.

His musing was abruptly interrupted as the air was rent asunder by what might well have been the soundtrack of a Hollywood blockbuster seeking an Oscar for the loudest film. Three bangs, which sounded like explosions, challenged Tony's ears and he was relieved that, whatever had happened, the train was still upright and seemingly on the track, despite, judging by the noise, it had skidded for some yards. By now he was the only passenger in the coach, others having departed at earlier stations, so had nobody with whom he could discuss what had happened.

Within a few minutes, an employee of the company strolled into Tony's carriage and apologised for what he described as a technical problem. That said, he was confident that there would be only a short delay before "we'll be on our way again". Tony found it impossible to believe that, following such a disastrous noise, progress would be made in the near future. Motivated by his desire to catch his flight, he was not prepared to accept what seemed like a bogus promise of progress.

Addressing the uniformed person he said "let me stop you in your tracks" and apologised for the pun before swiftly moving on as it was apparent that the man did not know what a pun was. He assured Tony that the delay was nothing to do with the track, "if you get my meaning sir, or a pun". He was confident in this because if a pun had been involved, he knew that he would have been told but he had never heard of a pun causing an accident. The passenger had something to say and clearly was determined to find out why the train had lost interest or ability in conveying him and any other fellow passengers, wherever they might be, from reaching their destinations. It might best to let him speak.

"I do a lot of travelling, not just here in the UK, including Scotland, Northern Ireland and let's not forget Wales, but abroad, in the USA and Eastern Europe mainly, on trains and planes" Tony said, trying to avoid smiling at his lie, "and I get fed up with hearing that kind of language which I know is imposed on you by unthinking management who are keen to avoid any responsibility and prefer secrecy to honesty in almost everything they do. I'm a paying passenger" and here he paused, almost implying that everyone else on the train might have failed to pay for their journey, "and I want to know what you really mean. All I know is that never in my life have I heard such a noise and I imagine that the engine has blown up, in which case what will happen to us? I have a plane to catch as I'm going to San Francisco on work."

"I went there once, on holiday, with my missus. Nice place I thought." Then, sensing that this international businessman meant business and that there was no more mention of puns, the emissary confessed. "I know where you're coming from sir…" Tony interrupted that that was because he had seen his ticket and continued "am I on the right track and that the engine has failed?"

"Let's put it this way, sir. We are on the part of the

line that is single track so, in that sense, you and the rest of us are on the wrong track. I don't want to speculate sir, that's above my pay level. All I can say, sir, is that we have a problem and that I've been told by my bosses to tell you that we shall soon be on our way."

Here he speculated that someone might have fallen on to the track and said "anyway, I'm afraid that we might be here for at least a little time. Tony's comment that he had to catch a plane merely produced a calming assurance that "I'm sure we'll be on our way soon sir."

Tony was certain that there would be a long delay and that he might miss his flight so when the official returned, he was not surprised to learn that the situation was very serious.

"The problem, sir, is that our engine has ceased to function, or to put it in day to day parlance, it has conked out."

Tony wanted to know what the company proposed to do. Could the engine driver fix the problem?

"I'm very worried I might miss my flight."

The official who now introduced himself as Fred, as he sensed that he and this passenger were going to spend some time together, shook his head.

"No, sir, there's nobody on this train that can fix the problem, and like gas companies that repair boilers, we don't carry any spares."

"So, presumably, a relief engine comes to rescue us?"

"No, that's the real problem. We're on a single track and there are trains in front and behind us queuing to join the single track but can't because we are in the way. Then any rescue engine leaving Waterloo would not be able to join us as there would be other trains in the queue waiting to move on to the single track which we are blocking. In a word, sir, I don't see how we are going to solve this until them who are bosses send a replacement engine from somewhere."

"Why can't they send coaches to rescue us?"

"Take a look sir, on one side there is a fast flowing river and on the other side there is a forest. I think you'll agree that's not very helpful. I don't know what is going to happen but what do I know, I'm only fit to look at tickets? To be blunt sir, I think that I'd better read out the announcement."

"Ladies and Gentlemen, this is your train manager As you will have noticed, we are no longer moving forward to our destination at this moment in time and this is because of a technical problem. I can assure you that we are doing all we can to overcome the problem and must apologise for any inconvenience. Meanwhile, a trolley will be passing through the train offering complimentary refreshment. As soon as I have any news, I'll pass it on. Once again, my apologies."

Tony growled to himself any inconvenience!! His life was being turned upside down and his chances of catching his plane were becoming more remote by the minute. Half an hour later, Fred took to the airways to offer renewed apologies and to admit that it would be some time before a rescue engine would be arriving and that because of 'the immediate terrain in this location at this moment in time'

the company regretted that passengers could not be
'evacuated'.

"Meanwhile, I shall be passing through the train with
forms that will allow you to apply for compensation."

Tony was not prepared to complete the form
immediately. It was clear that, worst of all, he would miss
his flight so he used his phone, which, to his surprise,
worked, to book overnight accommodation and to re-book
a flight. He also sent a long message to his employer
apologising and explaining that he was in effect, being held
captive on a train but he hoped to see them perhaps 24
hours later.

Eventually, a relief engine rescued the angry and
weary passengers. Unfortunately, the coach service from
Woking to Heathrow had finished for the day and Tony
had to queue for a taxi. By the time that he had booked in
to the hotel, he was tired and hungry. The complimentary
food, publicised by Fred, had been totally inadequate with
each passenger being restricted to just one sandwich. It was
time to ring his wife. She interrupted him almost before he
had completed asking her how she was.

"Your plane seems very quiet. Are the engines Rolls
Royces and where is that child that always sits next to you
and bawls her head off all the flight?"

As soon as he could speak, Tony's next effort to
communicate with his spouse, apparently, did not reach
home as Sheila asked if he said that he was going downstairs
to find something to eat?

"Don't they still serve you in your seat and is the
plane a double decker?"

Tony said that he was not in a plane and Sheila interrupted him immediately.

"Don't tell me that you lost your passport again or was it your boarding card?"

Tony asked her to give him a chance to speak and explained what had happened. He assured her that his seat to the States had been rebooked and he had sent an explanatory message to head office. He then told her that he was fine but very tired so wished her goodnight and rang off. He knew that the restaurant was now closed for the night but had noticed a machine on the ground floor that offered packets of crisps, sandwiches and biscuits and some oddly coloured drinks. The machine accepted Tony's money but refused to provide any sustenance despite being kicked twice in the slot.

Being on the verge of mental if not physical exhaustion, Tony had little difficulty In falling asleep. About an hour later he woke briefly and instantly recalled his dream. This was not unusual. In recent weeks, he had played cricket for England, being hung in the Middle Ages and had some remarkably pleasurable experiences to which he had not been treated in real life. However, recollections of the dreams, if not noted immediately, which was rare, never returned. He grabbed a notepad by the side of his bed, and wrote down a few bullet points of what had been a horrific and frightening dream. He had done this for some time, having read of a philosopher he could not remember, from a century he could not recall, who had done this and discovered in the morning that he had written "Men are polygamous and women are monogamous". It was thought at the time that this was a momentous discovery.

In his dream, Tony was in an aircraft, plunging ever faster towards the sea. The engines were screaming and the passengers, aware that they had but seconds to live, were seeking comfort in clinging on to friends and strangers alike. Some had already been injured as parts of the plane bounced around what was left of the cabin. A few had tried to make a final call to loved ones but lost control as the phones fell from their hands as the plane spun to its doom. It was truly terrifying.

Tony soon fell asleep again and he was to be dormant for a few more hours. He had asked the radio alarm to wake him at 8.00 and he had tuned in to Radio 4 for the *Today* programme. The headlines made him shiver.

"News is coming in that an aircraft, which took off late last evening from Heathrow, destined for San Francisco, has fallen into the Atlantic. It is feared that there are no survivors."

Trembling, he looked at the note that he had scribbled to himself during the night.

36.
The Halfway House

Carl Gilleard

One

Oblivious to the heavy rain, Harris stood transfixed by the flat tyre on his treasured SUV parked on the driveway. Nearby the AA patrolman was sourcing a replacement, wisely taking refuge from the elements in his van. It didn't take long and dragging himself from the vehicle, he called out:

'Treadwell's can do a change this morning if you go straight away. Reflating the tyre should see you there safely. It's not far and I'll follow you in case of a mishap. Okay?'

Urgency was paramount. Harris had spent weeks painstakingly planning the celebratory trip across the Pennines to the Lake District. Yesterday he valeted the car, checked the engine oil, windscreen wash levels and tyre pressures. One tyre required air, but he missed the cause, unlike the patrolman who quickly noticed the offending nail following a call out.   'Let's go then. If they're quick my wife and I can still reach Keswick in daylight. I'll let her know what's happening.'

Harris headed up the path to the modest semi-detached bungalow that had been home since their marriage twenty-five years ago. Edith was waiting anxiously at the front door. She knew the effort her husband had put into organising their silver wedding and how disappointed he would be if things didn't go according to plan.

He asked Edith to let the hotel know they would be late arriving and suggested she prepare a packed lunch for the journey. The patrolman having dealt with the tyre, backed his van on to the road and waited for Harris to lead the way.

Edith watched as the two vehicles set off towards town. Once out of sight and encouraged by a sudden gust of icy March wind, she headed inside.

*

The couple met at a mutual friend's wedding. Neither had a 'plus one' and sought solace in each other's company at the Wedding Breakfast, their friend tactfully seating them together. With inhibitions eased by free-flowing champagne, they opened-up on their lives. They had much in common, both were twenty-four, lacked siblings and worked for the council, she in the Registrar's Office and he in Treasury. Both enjoyed trips to the cinema, taking long walks and their own company. The evening ended with Harris tentatively suggesting they go for a walk together.

It wasn't love at first sight. A lengthy courtship was followed by a low-key wedding, the witnesses being the couple whose wedding they attended. Celebrations were limited to afternoon tea at Betty's Café in York after which the newlyweds took a taxi to the marital bungalow to spend their first night together. The honeymoon was delayed until July when they travelled by bus to Keswick for a week's camping on the shores of Derwentwater. Sadly, on the second night they discovered the tent was no match for the Cumbrian weather and torrential rain put paid to their plans. The following morning, sodden clothes were packed into equally sodden rucksacks, the tent dumped in a waste bin and the downcast couple returned home. En route, Harris promised to make amends with a return trip, staying in the resort's finest hotel in a room with views of the lake; a hastily made promise quickly forgotten until Harris uncharacteristically suggested a return to the Lakes would be the perfect way to celebrate their forthcoming silver wedding. Without children or parents to consider they could 'Do whatever we want. Just the two of us!'

The tyre change took longer than anticipated and it was one o'clock before Harris reversed the car up the driveway. Edith had stacked luggage in the hallway ready to load up. Harris insisted on packing the cases in sequence, unaware that his wife had added another holdall. Confusion reigned as he kept removing the luggage Edith placed in the boot. It was still raining as they skipped back and forth, hallway to car boot, and back again. Eventually Harris solved the three-dimensional puzzle by placing the extra holdall on the back seat. Not an entirely satisfactory solution but it would have to do. The packed lunch was placed in the rear footwell. Double-checking they had locked the house they departed, two hours behind schedule.

Bypassing the city centre was slow owing to emergency roadworks. Harris preferred to drive in silence while Edith, who never drove, was content to sit back and watch the world go by, the peace broken only by the whirring of windscreen wipers. Once through the roadworks, traffic moved more smoothly. They were now three hours behind schedule. 'With luck we can make up time on the open road,' Harris optimistically predicted.

To an extent he was right. Traffic heading northwest was thinning out. The ascent into the Pennine hills was gradual but the rain had turned to sleet much to Edith's consternation. 'The weather's deteriorating Harris, should we be doing this?'

Not one to concede defeat or alter plans, Harris responded, 'Don't worry, the car can handle this stuff. It's not settling, and we're not alone.'

True, they were in a convoy but at each passing village numbers dwindled. The sleet had turned to snow and to distract Edith, he enquired if she had contacted the hotel.

'Yes, they said not to worry. There's always room service if we don't make dinner.' The time was now approaching five and the night was drawing in.

A prolonged silence followed as Harris concentrated on maintaining a safe distance from the car in front. When its driver braked, he braked. As the road weaved its way upwards, conditions were deteriorating fast. A combination of the car's speed and a swirling wind made visibility difficult. Harris found it mesmerising and kept blinking hard and breathing deeply to maintain focus. Encouraged by having company he refused to consider turning back.

Another few miles and the convoy reduced to just four vehicles; ominously nothing was passing the other way. At the next village the lead car stopped, leaving Harris at the front. Turning the headlights on to full beam, he was guided by cats' eyes on roadside marker posts. Road and sky merged into a blanket white canvas, falling snow pounding the windscreen, the wipers screeching in protest.

Harris ploughed on into the night. According to the sat-nav another village lay a mile ahead, a road sign reminding travellers to drive carefully. Drystone walls gave way to stone cottages, twinkling house lights reminding Edith they were far from the warmth and safety of their bungalow.

Beyond the village expanses of barren featureless moorland offered no defence against the elements. Visibility was down to a few metres and Harris, hands firmly gripping the steering wheel, leaned forward straining to spot the way ahead.

Edith read Harris like a book and had spotted the mood change. Observing the grim facial gestures, taut body and laboured breathing she saw he was competing with the weather conditions and that worried her, a lot.

Suddenly a sheep appeared on the road ahead, frozen in the car's headlights. Edith shrieked as Harris instinctively braked and swerved, the car careering out of control eventually bumping to a halt on the snow-covered verge inches away from a marker post. The pair sat in shocked silence processing what had happened.

Harris spoke first: 'Where the hell did that come from?'

Noting the rare curse, Edith replied: 'I've no idea but at least you missed it. Are you okay?'

'Shaken and very relieved. We were lucky. See how

close we came to hitting that post.'

Selecting reverse gear, he teased the accelerator, but the car slid further off the road. Downbeat, he turned the engine off followed by the windscreen wipers and headlights. The only sound, a constant wailing wind.

In the murky darkness Harris was lost in thought. The overwhelming sense was one of relief. His obdurate ambition to reach the hotel that evening was over; the battle had ended in defeat courtesy of a wayward sheep. Sat there staring out at a hostile wilderness, he questioned his resolve in pursuing a journey that had clearly become more precarious by the minute. What had got into him?

He turned to Edith who had sat in silence throughout his epiphany and asked if she was hungry?

'Yes, and thirsty,' she said, reaching into the rear footwell to retrieve lunch. She had packed cheese and pickle sandwiches, chocolate digestives and coffee. 'What do you fancy?'

Harris, ever practical, suggested they ration themselves to a shared sandwich and a couple of biscuits. Despite the paucity of the meal, it raised their spirits.

Next, they donned their outdoor kit for warmth, waterproofs, thermal socks, boots, gloves, hats and scarves from the holdall on the back seat. Energized by the exercise, Harris left the car to check on their situation. the air chill taking his breath away. The attempt at reversing had left deep muddy rut marks beneath the wheels. Stepping round the back of the car he noticed a stream running along a gully, a short step from Edith's door.

Back inside he described their perilous situation to

Edith. 'It would be risky to try and reverse our way out. We could easily end up in the gully. We need another vehicle with a tow rope to drag us back on to the road – and that's unlikely to happen tonight."

Edith accepted the gloomy diagnosis. Still, they had refreshments and were well wrapped up against the cold. She checked her mobile for a signal but without success. The sat-nav was also disconnected.

'We'll have to stay warm and keep ourselves entertained,' she said turning on the radio, the familiar theme-tune to The Archers filling the car. The storyline was about the disappearance of a church collecting box but Harris's mind was elsewhere. How were they going to survive the night? He could turn the engine on for a few minutes at a time but would it be enough to combat the Arctic conditions?

A threatening dampness crept into the car. A further intake of lukewarm coffee and biscuits did little to raise spirits. It was now nine o'clock. Harris took a set of OS maps from the glove compartment selecting one and spreading it across the steering wheel. By torchlight he highlighted their position.

'Here's us, and there's the pub I planned to stop at for lunch, the Halfway House,' he said pointing to a PH sign.

Edith was askance. 'You're not suggesting we leave the car, are you?'

Harris chose his words carefully, 'Listen, we've no idea how long we might be stranded. There's no passing traffic, so the road must be impassable. It could be hours, perhaps days, before we are rescued. It'll be challenging, yes, but worth it to reach shelter. It's only a mile away and we can be there in an hour, perhaps sooner. Let's be positive.'

Edith remained unconvinced but knew her husband would persist until he had persuaded her, so reluctantly she agreed and prayed they were doing the right thing

*

Having filled a backpack with the remaining food and drink they were ready to depart.

'We'll walk in single file Edith. I'll lead, you follow in my footsteps to avoid the worst of the wind. Okay with that?'

Edith nodded her assent. Covering their faces with scarves they set off, Harris counting footsteps ten at a time. Reaching a hundred he glanced back over Edith's shoulder, the abandoned car was no longer visible.

On they went. Another hundred steps, another pause. Somehow, they stayed upright despite the treacherous conditions underfoot. Edith could feel the first signs of fatigue; her legs like lead weights, her breathing heavy. Ahead of them the road dropped away sharply to an ancient stone bridge straddling a watercourse. With the bridge providing respite from the wind, Harris beckoned Edith to kneel behind the stonework for shelter. From the backpack, he removed a sandwich which Edith ignored. She was slumped on her haunches shivering, her lips and skin blue in the torchlight. He tried stimulating her interest by telling her how many words the Inuit people used to describe snow, but she showed no interest. Her speech was slow and slurred.

'Can we just stay here and rest? I can't go any further.'

Harris recognised the danger signs of hypothermia, yet they were still half a mile from the inn. He had to motivate Edith to move and fast. Reaching out, he pulled her up.

'Time to go. We're almost there, one last effort and we can relax.'

And with that they set off again, this time he linked arms to bear as much of her weight as possible.

Uphill they scrambled until once more they faced the biting wind, footsteps shortening to a mere shuffle. Each second seemed like a minute, each minute an hour. Progress was painfully slow. Abandoning the counting routine, Harris focused on keeping Ellen upright fearing that if she fell down she would stay down. The physical effort was telling on him too yet every few steps he shone the torch in the hope of catching sight of the inn.

Miraculously, it stopped snowing and visibility improved. A dark mass appeared out of the gloom, but Harris hesitated to mention it in case his imagination was playing tricks. A few more steps and a large stone building with mullion windows, a porch and a swinging sign advertising 'The Halfway House' took shape. His relief was tempered by the lack of lighting, the one encouraging sign being the sweet smell of burning wood permeating the air.

Two

Writers of Ottery

The weary travellers sought refuge in the porch, Edith collapsing on to a wooden bench. Looking up she pleaded, 'Try the door Harris, please.'

He wrapped his near frozen fingers around the brass doorknob, struggling to turn it. Using a shoulder as a lever, he pushed harder, and the door sprang open taking him with it. Inside, the bar was in darkness except for the glow of a lit woodstove on the far wall.

'Hello! Is anybody there?' he called out.
Edith, raising herself from the bench, crept up beside him when a scratchy male voice came from the darkness: 'Over here by the fire.'

The pair moved cautiously towards the stove set in an inglenook. Adjusting their eyes to the gloom, they spotted three leather armchairs encircling the fireplace and a low table hosting a bottle and three glass tumblers. In the far chair sat a shadowy figure, long spindly legs outstretched, shoeless feet touching the hearth. It was difficult to pick out any features other than he was tall and wearing military fatigues.

'Put your wet clothes over there, they'll soon dry out what with the roaring fire.'

The pair did as instructed, then sat down, Edith deliberately choosing the chair furthest from the stranger, but close to the fire.

'What a relief to find the inn open,' said Harris. 'We abandoned our car a mile back.'

The stranger was staring into the fire. 'Aye, it's a blessing right enough. Been a long-established tradition to provide refuge to those that get caught out by the weather.'

'Well, we are very grateful. Thanks again,' responded Harris.

'It's not me you should be thanking, it's landlady.'

'It's not your pub then?'

'If only! No, I'm in the same boat as you. The blizzard took us by surprise.'

'So, where is the landlady?' enquired a suspicious Edith.

'Upstairs asleep, reckon. Wouldn't be expecting anyone this late. Place was in darkness when I arrived.'

'That's very trusting. We could help ourselves to, well, whatever takes our fancy,' suggested an incredulous Edith.

'Aye you could, so long as you settle-up in the morning. Only there's no electricity. Must have been a power cut so we've a limited choice, nothing hot or from the pumps. I'm on the Talisker single malt, a tribute to the landlady hailing from Skye. That's it on the table. I've had a couple of snifters already. Help yourselves.'

Harris had enjoyed sampling Talisker's distinctive sweet and smokey notes before. Leaning over he poured a couple of generous measures and handed one to Ellen.

'It not right,' she complained, 'helping ourselves.'

'Don't worry lass, landlady's husband will be up early to tend his sheep. She'll be down soon after when you can settle up. As I said, it's a tradition.'

'You're from these parts then?' Edith enquired.

'Born a couple miles away down in the valley. Pub cricket team's pitch was in my village. I was a half-decent fast bowler as a lad and the pub asked me to play for them. After the match, the players came here for refreshments.

Had my first pint of bitter here. Any roads, how come you were travelling over the moor today of all days?'

Harris was about to pose the same question but decided that by going first it might encourage the stranger to open-up, so he quickly described their ordeal.

The stranger listened attentively. 'Well at least you made it. I'm Arnold by the way, Arnie for short.'

'Oh, like Arnold Schwarzenegger?' Edith chipped in.

'Who? Never heard of him.'

'You must have. He's a famous movie star and politician in America.'

Harris wanted to get the conversation back on track. 'Anyway, I'm Harris and my wife is Edith.'

'Nice to meet you, Harry.'

'It's Harris actually, my mother's maiden name.'

'If you insist. Harry's more friendly though, don't you think?'

Edith was aware of the sensitivity surrounding her husband's name. 'I like Harris, it suits him,' she said, smiling at her husband.

Arnie fell silent.

'So, Arnie, how did you get here?' Harris probed.

'Shank's pony.'

'You walked? Why would you go walking in this weather?'

Arnie was clearly conflicted. Weighing his words carefully, he explained.

'I enlisted in the Lancashire Fusiliers and made it to corporal but when my unit was disbanded, I switched to the Parachute Regiment. Five of us were on a jump exercise today. We were dropped on the moors with orders to reach the trig point on Beacon Hill and then continue to a recce at 16.00 hours before returning to base. There should have been six of us, but the wireless op was granted compassionate leave to visit his wife in hospital, lucky devil.'

He broke off for a few moments, as if to collect his thoughts, and then resumed, 'The forecast was for squally showers turning to snow later by which time we should have been safely back in camp. Our pilot raised concerns about high winds but the commanding officer insisted we proceed. He joked that lacking radio contact would be more realistic. I was the last to jump and, sod's law, drifted well away from the others.'

'Knowing the landscape, I headed to where the others should have waited, but they'd scarpered. I made my way to Beacon Hill but saw no sign of them. Conditions were dreadful, driving snow, sub-zero temperatures and only this uniform for protection. Half froze I was. Daylight was fading and I was in danger of spending the night alone on the moor with no rations. I had two options as I saw it. The chief would expect me to find my way back to camp by heading for the main road three miles west and then thumb a lift. Or I could head east and be guaranteed shelter here. I chose the latter option and the gamble paid off.'

'Have you let your unit know you are safe?' asked a concerned Edith.

'Nah. It'll be right as ninepence. I'll lose my stripes but at least I'm alive. Think that calls for another dram, don't you Harry?'

Harris topped up the glasses. It seemed to him that

Arnie was rehearsing his lines for when he had to account for his actions.

'What do you think happened to your comrades Arnie?'

'No bloody idea. They disappeared into thin air. Didn't spend any time looking for me, did they?'

There was a hint of anger in Arnie's voice, or was it regret?

Ignoring the question, Harris turned to Edith to ask if she liked the whisky but found her curled up in the armchair, sleeping.

'Looks like my wife's out for the count Arnie. Perhaps we should get some rest too. It's been an exhausting day. We can chat again in the morning'

Arnie seemed preoccupied. Harris took the opportunity to take a closer look at the stranger. His face was taut and sallow, eyes deep-set giving him a haunted look. He hadn't shaved recently or combed his unkempt hair.

Several drams of whisky and the heat from the fire had a soporific effect on Harris. Reluctantly, he gave in to an overwhelming desire to close his eyes and drift off. The mysterious soldier was the only one not to succumb.

Three

Edith was a habitual early riser. She woke at six-thirty and tried to get her bearings. The blazing fire told her she was not at home and the stiffness in her muscles indicated she had not slept in a bed. In the half-light she spotted Harris

193

slumped in the chair next to her. She rose slowly, stretched and reached out to give him a gentle shake.

'Harris,' she whispered, 'are you awake?'

She repeated the question twice before getting a response.

'What's the time?' he asked, stifling a yawn.

'It's almost seven and someone's up and about.'

Harris glanced to his right, but Arnie wasn't there, nor was his chair. Then he noticed the half empty bottle and two empty tumblers on the table. Behind him there was the sound of movement. Turning he saw a woman advancing towards him carrying two steaming mugs.

'Gave me quite a shock finding you two spark-out. Sorry to wake you but my day starts early. I'm Janice by the way, landlady of this fine establishment.'

Edith reacted first. 'We were so grateful to find the inn open. It was a life saver.'

'Yes, about that. I'm certain I locked up before going to bed. Didn't you find my note pinned to the door asking visitors to go to the back entrance and ring the bell?'

Harris described their arrival. 'We were greeted by a soldier who said he'd arrived shortly before us. He was sat by the fire and invited us to join him.'

'A soldier, really? Where's he now?' asked Janice.

'We thought it was strange too. He said he was a paratrooper on an exercise that fell apart.'

'His name was Arnie and he said he was a local,' Edith chipped in.

Janice placed the mugs on the table and in the same motion lifted the whisky bottle, examining it's contents.

'Seems you had quite a session last night. This bottle was full. Maybe you imagined the soldier.' She meant it as a joke but could tell her guests were unamused.

Defensively, Edith explained that the disappearing soldier had recommended the whisky as a power cut ruled out hot drinks.

'Umm. Well, firstly we have our own generator, so we're not reliant on the grid and, secondly, it's odd he selected Talisker as there's not much call for it here.'

Harris recalled Arnie telling them it was a tradition established by a previous landlady who was from Skye.

'There was a Scottish landlady but I'm a Lancashire lass through and through. Anyway, no harm done and thanks for keeping the fire alight, that's saved me a job this morning. In return, how about I prepare you a cooked breakfast? Feel free to use the soap and towels I've put in the restrooms to freshen up and I'll have breakfast ready in, say, twenty minutes?' she suggested, glancing at her wristwatch.

Licensees are good judges of character and Janice was adept at spotting con artists. While she couldn't explain the unlocked door, the disappearing soldier or the episode with the whisky, she was convinced that these visitors were genuine if gullible types.

*

As Edith and Harris finished breakfast, Janice joined them

at the table. She had brought a fresh cafetiere of coffee and three mugs.

'Mind if I join you?' Without waiting for a reply, she sat down, 'Sorry I doubted you earlier. I've been reflecting on what you said, and reckon your mysterious soldier was a chancer who somehow got in. Your arrival probably stopped him taking whatever took his fancy. It's fashionable to wear army fatigues these days so I doubt he was a soldier. Anyway, he's gone, so no harm done.'

The relief on her guests' faces was a picture.

'Jim, my husband, is out tending the animals and spotted your car. He'll take you to it later this morning and tow you out. The sun's shining and a thaw is setting in, so he reckons you'll be away by lunchtime. In the meantime, why not relax in the lounge.'

Jim's prediction was accurate. He and Harris towed the abandoned car to the inn where there was a parked snowplough. The crew were inside tucking into bowls of Lancashire hotpot. They advised Harris to go easy for the first few miles after which road conditions were almost back to normal.

Settling a modest bill, the travellers thanked Janice and Jim and were on their way.

Four

The onward journey was delightful, a fusion of sun and snow transforming the landscape into an alpine scene. Arriving in Keswick the thaw was well and truly underway.

The hotel generously upgraded the couple's

accommodation so they could celebrate their silver wedding in style. Over the next few days, the Lakes enjoyed wall to wall sunshine and the twosome took full advantage, climbing Catbells and circumnavigating Buttermere. They also squeezed in trips to the Pencil Museum and The Theatre by the Lake.

Eventually though, it was time to return home. They took the same route back, arriving at the Halfway House at lunchtime. During their stay in Keswick they agreed not to talk about what happened at the inn but before departing, Ellen strolled into town while Harris loaded the car, returning with a bouquet of spring flowers as a thank you gesture to Janice and Jim.

The atmosphere inside the inn was buzzing. Janice was behind the bar and greeted them with a smile. 'Well, this is a surprise. Fancy seeing you again. How was Keswick?'

Ellen placed the bouquet on the bar. 'These are for you. A token of our gratitude for taking care of us last week.'

'They're lovely, but you shouldn't have. All part of the service. You must stay for lunch and try the hotpot. Find a table and I'll take your order once I've put the flowers in water.'

The only available seats meant sharing a table with two elderly men.

*

Arthur Barrow and his son Barry visited the inn every

197

Wednesday. They booked the same table each week, a routine Arthur knew would soon end. A lifetime of working at the nearby quarry left him with silicosis and a recent check-up confirmed it had progressed to lung cancer. It was a tribute to Arthur's strength of will that he was still getting out and about.

Barry also worked at the quarry, but an industrial accident resulted in him leaving to build a successful taxi business. Now retired he spent time with his dad, taxiing him around. The Wednesday routine was well established, pick dad up from the care home, drive to the inn, have lunch and enjoy people watching. It was a bonus if others shared their table, Arthur loving a good natter despite struggling to breathe. Today he was in luck.

'How do. Passing through, are we?' Arthur enquired of the strangers as they sat down. Before they could respond, he spoke again. ' I'm eighty-eight you knows, and I've been drinking here for over seventy years. That's right, isn't it Barry?'

Barry nodded and smiled at the new guests. 'Excuse dad. He can't help himself. Wants to know everyone's business, don't you?'

'We're heading home to Yorkshire,' replied Harris. 'We were stranded here last Friday actually. Trapped in the snowstorm on our way to the Lakes.'

'Someone has to live there I suppose,' quipped Arthur. 'So that were you two. A bit risky abandoning your car in that blizzard. Lots of folk have been caught out over the years. Not so much recently though what with global warming. Aye, there's been some changes over my lifetime,' he reflected, gazing out of the window and catching his breath

This was an entrée Edith couldn't resist. 'What sort of changes?' she asked, hoping to engage Arthur in revealing more.

Arthur didn't need encouraging. 'You can say that again. I left school at fourteen and worked at yonder quarry. A wagon ferried us here in relays for our dinners. We had half an hour to down our food and get back before they docked our wages. Hard times. This place has seen lots of publicans come and go, but Janice is the best and her hotpots are to die for.'

Edith continued her probing. 'Why did you work at the quarry Arthur?'

'There wasn't much else other than farming and that were badly paid, still is. So I chose quarrying. And I didn't fancy being out on the moor in all weathers.'

'You know the moors well then?'

'Aye, as a lad me and my mates would camp overnight next to a stream. It were an adventure but one Easter we were stopped from doing it. Never did it again.'

'Why, what happened?'

Arthur frowned as he cast his mind back. 'It were a long time ago, the army were involved. That's right, five soldiers out on manoeuvres disappeared in a snow-storm. Caused a right stink. Four of them died from exposure, the fifth, a local chap, he were never found. I'd be about thirteen and the thought of stumbling across human remains put me off tramping over them moors for good.'

'That's terrible. You were thirteen you say, so it would

be 1943 when it happened?' Harris raised an eyebrow at Edith's forthright questioning.

'I left school a year later, so aye, thirteen. Why does the year matter, lass?'

'It seems such a needless loss of life, soldiers out on a routine exercise. There must be ways of finding people who go missing on the moors.'

Barry chipped in. 'Today there's a local mountain rescue team on call for when folk get into difficulties but there's still the odd emergency. People don't appreciate how quickly the weather can deteriorate.'

'Don't we know it,' muttered Harris.

Edith had one last question for Arthur who was visibly tiring. 'You don't happen to remember the name of the soldier who went missing do you, him being local?'

Arthur shook his head. 'Like I said lass, it were a long time since.'

At this moment Janice came over to take their order. 'I see you've met our longest serving customer. I hope you're behaving yourself Arthur. Another pint you two?'

'No thanks Janice, we must be on our way,' said Barry getting to his feet. 'Nice to meet you both. Safe journey home.'

He waited while Arthur struggled to his feet and then helped him to the door.

Minutes later Edith and Harris were tucking into Janice's famous hotpot.

Lunch over and farewells made, the pair headed for the carpark. Once inside the SUV Harris turned to his wife.

'You certainly had the bit between your teeth in there Edith. Your questioning of poor old Arthur was almost forensic. What were you up to?'

Ellen feigned innocence at first but under pressure she admitted she couldn't resist probing into what had transpired on the moor all those years ago.

'I know we agreed not to talk about Arnie in Keswick but that didn't stop me thinking about him. Was he, as Janice suggested, a chancer who happened to be passing by, or could he have been a ghost?' There, for the first time she had used the word they had carefully skirted round since meeting Arnie.

Before Harris could protest, she continued:

'Remember when you went to recover the car? Well, left to my own devices I looked around the bar area. On the wall opposite the woodstove there was a collection of photographs. Some were of celebrity visitors, soap stars and the like, others of staff members. There was also a few of the inn's cricket team down the years. I noticed one dated 1938 and on the back row stood a tall lean chap who could have been a young Arnie and the listing named him as A. Deadman.' Harris started to interrupt but Edith put her hands up to stop him. 'I knew you would be sceptical, so I snapped it on my phone.'

She showed the image to a perplexed Harris. Shocked at what his wife's investigation had revealed, he was dumbfounded.

Edith had already considered the implications of her findings and was ready to share them.

'If we go back in there and claim we spent the night

with a ghost we would face ridicule and to what end? It would be an utter waste of breath trying to convince sceptics. Think how we would react, Harris. So why not keep it to ourselves?'

Relief showed on Harris's face.

'That makes sense. After all we were the only ones who actually saw Arnie. You're right Edith, time to move on. Let's head for home,' and with that he turned the ignition on.

Edith smiled to herself. So far, so good, she thought. She would choose a better time and place to tell Harris of her pledge to explore the circumstances surrounding the tragic demise of Corporal A. Deadman and his comrades. An initial trawl of the web conducted in the small hours when Harris slept had failed to uncover a single reference to the moorland tragedy 75 years ago.

However, it did offer several ways of accessing army personnel records. Her first task would be to find a member of the Deadman family to endorse her actions. All in a day's work for an assistant registrar. Content with the progress made, she sat back and relaxed, enjoying the passing scenery and relishing the challenge ahead.

About the Authors

J.E.Hall has written several contemporary novels since 2014, exploring aspects of extremism and terrorism in gripping stories. In 2022, together with Ottery artist Mike Bird, they produced 'The Modern Trooper', an illustrated poem based on Coleridge's Rime of the Ancient Mariner. John is currently working on an Ottery based novel set in Tudor times. His website is https://www.jehallauthor.com

Cynthea Gregory initially trained as a Design and Technology teacher. She left teaching to join her husband working in France. There she combined two of her hobbies, photography and cookery, to write three cookbooks in French. On returning to Britain, she has self-published two novels. Website: cynthea.gregory@gmx.com

James Armstrong in 2020 published 'Between Painting Room and Paradise': a biography of the landscape painter, John Constable. A year later, he published a poetry collection with illustrations, 'Drawn Together'. He is currently researching and writing a chronicle of the construction of a remarkable, Chinese, Han Period tomb, discovered in 1968.

Graham Bishop has written a series of international

detective thrillers all with the theme of combatting the theft of works of art. Locations in France, Greece, Italy, Morocco, England and Scotland. He has also written a series of self teach language guides for French and German. His website is http://www.vidocqpress.com

Melanie Barrow turned to creative writing partly as therapy for long covid. She's had poems, non-fiction, flash fiction and short stories published in magazines and websites such as The Lady, Yours Fiction, Syncopation Literary Journal and 101 words. She was awarded 2nd prize in the Ottery Literary Festival and is hoping to find the time to start her first novel.

Richard Lappas has worked as a National newspaper photographer across 40 years covering the south west. He wrote an autobiography 'More by Good Luck than Judgement' in 2016. He now writes children's adventure books including the 'Adventure @ Muffin Bay' series and other projects.

Helen Connor was introduced to creative writing during illness, finding the process enormously cathartic.
As a counsellor Helen then used writing as a therapy with her clients leading her to begin an MSc in creative writing for therapeutic purposes. She writes poems for her own interest and for fun.

Ruth MacGregor. Poetry is her preferred writing style and she find nature something that inspires her. Her work was in pædiatrics and is now as a play therapist and she finds it hard to give time to writing. Joining the Ottery Writers group has been stimulating and encouraging..

Tony Dowling says his favourite writing is rhyming poetry. He draws his material from friends with theological leanings, from science, astronomy, the Forces and teaching construction and civil engineering. His aspiration is to write a book to help people to understand structural mechanics to the level of understanding the moment of inertia or the second moment of area.

Grenville Gilbert Graduated in Law at the University of Exeter in 1971. He has been writing poems of a religious and philosophic nature for 45 years. He was Churchwarden on 3 occasions at Ottery St Mary Parish Church, Devon.

David Kerr moved to Ottery St Mary from China. Originally a resident of East London, David and his daughter Maya quickly learned to appreciate the east Devon countryside and the strong community bonds of the small town. David writes commercially.

Anthology

Carl Gilleard OBE A constant thread running through Carl's career, spanning 50 years, was that of being a communicator. He has, among other things, been an editor, scriptwriter, public speaker, author of educational books and broadcaster. Now retired, he writes purely for the pleasure of being inventive with words.

Simon Cornish is a professional animator who works and lives in the beautiful city of Copenhagen – which lends a visual, and slightly Nordic, approach to his writing. He has published short and medium fiction, created a number of fantasy game books and is currently working on a speculative fiction novel or three.

Mary Hewlett writes largely autobiographical work and uses her nosiness/people watching skills to observe every day situations and characters. She cites Alan Bennett, Victoria Wood and Jane Austen as her heroes and Hugh Jackman bringing her Cadburys as her dream.

Philip Algar was an economist before becoming a freelance editor, journalist and occasional broadcaster. He has written 15 books about the wartime Merchant Navy, Crisis Management and satires on current life as well as a collection of short stories.

Bob Sillitoe started writing in 2013. An undiscovered gift lying dormant. Now a major part of his life. Romance the genre and for an engineer a strange but addictive mixture. The Ottery Writers group has been a key motivator when it comes to writing and editing and following the process right through to publishing.

Sim Taylor is fortunate to have been born and raised in Devon. She spent her childhood in the fields and hedgerows close to her home in the suburbs of Exeter. Her writing stays faithful to her Devonshire heritage. This is her first short story and is a retelling of a tale about færie ointment much told in various forms throughout the UK.

In addition to the above, the 2022 Ottery Literary Festival Prizewinning entries by other authors are included in the Anthology.

Afterword

We hope you have enjoyed reading our work. As you will no doubt have gathered we are a group of enthusiasts with no major publisher backing us or editorial board professionals checking our spellings and grammar. It is what it is!

As a group of friends we don't have a formal constitution or elected officers or a budget. Any funds we contribute come from amongst ourselves goes to cover the cost of room hire and refreshments. This means all our energies are in one direction – to encourage local writers. We ought not to finish this book without acknowledging encouragement given by both Ottery Town Council and the Curious Otter Bookshop. Thank you!

If you enjoyed this book please tell friends, family, colleagues and use your own social media to give it a plug. Reviews through our website are always welcome and if you want to contact us then please do so.

Our meetings generally take place from 7-9pm on the second Monday of each month in the Town Council Meeting in The Square. We always seek to offer newcomers a warm welcome, so why not come along?

Website: https://otterywriters.wordpress.com

Writers of Ottery

Anthology

Printed in Great Britain
by Amazon

24282186R00119